AIRSHIP 27 PRODUCTIONS

Sherlock Holmes: The Baron's Revenge
© 2012 Gary Lovisi

Interior llustrations © 2012 Rob Davis
Cover illustration © 2012 Rob Davis & Shane Evans

Editor: Ron Fortier
Associate Editor: Charles Saunders
Production and design by Rob Davis.

Published by
Airship 27 Productions
www.airship27.com
www.airship27hangar.com

ISBN-13: 978-0615594439
ISBN-10: 0615594433

Printed in the United States of America

10 9 8 7 6 5 4 3 2 1

Sherlock Holmes

The Baron's Revenge

by
Gary Lovisi

Preface:
A Letter To The Reader

*A*s many of Watson's long suffering readers are aware, the good doctor could not resist the urge to put pen to paper to chronicle what he considered the most memorable adventures of my consulting detective career.

While I often derided Watson's literary efforts as pandering to sensationalism in the popular press and chided him for overly melodramatic narration, I must admit that he, in his 'little stories,' was sincere in doing his utmost to examine those special gifts and talents he attributed to me, and documented my success in solving crimes that baffled the official police.

In the past, Watson had mentioned that he was loath to write a follow-up to any case he had previously chronicled. Truth be told, for most cases there seemed little reason to revisit the original story — no pretext to present an update concerning the primary persons from the original crime. That may have been true — until now.

I believe the story you are about to read will add a deeper dimension to the original case Watson and I first encountered back in the Autumn of 1902. It is one I allowed to be published in **The Strand** magazine last year under the title "The Adventure of the Illustrious Client."

Now, in this new narrative, I present a continuation of that case. It includes most of the principals who were part of the original 1902 case and follows their lives and activities with deadly results three years later. Moreover, this case is one that had dire consequences for Watson and myself. We found ourselves trapped in a diabolical plot created to put an end — once and for all — to the life of my good friend Doctor John H. Watson — as well *as to my own life and career.*

 Now in my later years and in retirement, it is with a heavy heart that I once again take pen to paper to chronicle one of my cases. This time I omit all laudatory nonsense to concentrate on the case at hand which included several severe errors on my part. Watson was always after me to write-up my own cases, so in his memory, I have taken pen in hand once again. While I often chided my good friend about his embellishments of my talents and adventures, I must admit that he was correct all along on one key ingredient. It is far easier for one to critique a writer's meager efforts, than it is for one to write them himself. How well I have done here, I shall leave to you, gentle reader.

 Sherlock Holmes
 The Downs
 Sussex, England, 1926

Chapter 1:
Kitty and Porky

The streets were dark, the mood darker. The narrow lanes and byways were the usual traps where ruffians plied their grim trade and easy women went about making hard money.

Shinwell "Porky" Johnson was one of the toughest of those who inhabited the area; a coarse, ruddy-faced lout who looked wasted from sin, only his vivid black eyes let on to those acute enough to notice that he was no mere lowly wastrel but a fellow who possessed a cunning and dangerous mind. It was a professional criminal mind.

Johnson walked the streets boldly here, without fear, for these were his streets, this was his part of London; the part none of those reeking of class or culture hardly knew existed. He went up to one of the hovels down the bend, over to No. 67 and knocked heavily.

"That you, Porky?" a soft female voice answered from within.

"You know it is, dearie."

"Well. It's unlocked, so come on in."

Johnson shook his head in consternation and mild chagrin. He'd told the daft broad a dozen times, "Keep the door locked! Always lock the door." But she was as hard-headed as he was — perhaps even more so, if that were possible — so he knew there was nothing left to be said on the matter. He entered the small rented room carefully but with a growing sense of excitement at what he would find.

Once inside, his eyes feasted upon the image of a truly lovely woman. She was slim of waist but flame-like, a fiery beauty, intense of face and still youthful despite the severe damage done to her years before. He did not even want to think about that now, as his eyes feasted lovingly upon the many parts of her that were still lovely and…undamaged.

"I know," she mused wickedly in a high-pitched Cockney accent, "you always tell me to lock the door. I tell you, I does it when I remember, Porky,

Once inside, his eyes feasted upon the image of a truly lovely woman.

but I do not think it matters much any more after all these years."

Johnson smiled, he couldn't help it really, rough lout that he was he'd always been keen on Kitty, and she knowing that, had always used him as a trusted agent and sometimes friend. A bond had grown up between them over their years of criminal activities, a partnership, a measure of respect to be sure. However, especially in the matter of the last three years, Porky saw himself more and more as Kitty's agent, protector, and though he'd never admit it and dared not tell her of his feelings — her lover. Of a sorts…

"I still think it might be…prudent…"

"Prudent, you say?" and she laughed gaily, allowing the lovely side of her body to show which mesmerized him by its beauty. The side of her body wracked by the terrible damage was not now visible so that for the barest instant Johnson was blessed to see an image of Kitty as she had once been, before all her misfortune had begun. She looked simply lovely, a fire-red wench that could still burn desire into any man's heart. Kitty looked at the man before her and just laughed gaily, "By cripes, is that a new word you just learned today? Prudent, you say! Oh my!"

Johnson blushed, and it took a lot to make this street tough show any measure of sensitivity, but Kitty knew just how to do it to him, "I just mean to say…"

"I know, Porky, but it is all right now. I am sure of it. He's gone and back home, very ill I hear, and I hope he's dying. Good riddance! Three years have passed so it's all best left forgotten. I want to forget it all as well, if I can. I do try, though it is difficult — a fight every day it is. I want to forget it all. I think it is better that way."

"I know you don't like to think about it," he said softly, knowing only too well the pain she had gone through. The pain that she was still going through that wracked her spirit and soul every day.

"I wish to erase it all from my mind. You understand? You know what I went through," she stated, looked away, then she looked back and gave him a wry grin. "Anyways, now I'm out of gaol and just a working girl again. Now I needs me money."

Johnson shook his head visibly irritated. They'd had this discussion before as well, but he was determined to go through it all again with her if it might cause her a change of mind. "You don't need to do this business any longer, Kitty. I told you I'd take care of you," he said it softly in his own gruff manner, but he meant it with all his heart.

His words touched the woman before him with a warmness she rarely felt any longer. As hard as she was, as hard as she had become, Kitty Winter had a soft spot for her Porky. She knew he'd be true to her. She smiled at him and he savored that smile.

"You don't believe me?" he said boldly, subdued, a rush of redness to his face.

"Of course I believes you, silly, but there is more to things than just what you are thinking."

Johnson shook his head. "I don't like it."

"I know. But what then, if we do it your way? You stealing and putting yourself in danger for me. The peelers coming for you in the dead of night and then you being sent to gaol — or worse — the hangman's rope. See, I knows your bad temper, Porky. While you treat me like the princess I am surely not...I knows you'll not be so gentle with anyone who comes between you and freedom...or a handful of gold..."

"Don't talk like that!"

"It's nothing but truth. I'm a whore, Porky. I admit it. I have become a whore and I sell meself for money, but for good money, eh? Gold crowns, sovereigns and the like."

Johnson dropped his head low. He did not like this kind of talk, he did not like to bare the truth between them out in the open like this, and the truth of who and what they were. What they had become.

It was all because of — that man!

"It's all right, Porky," she cooed softly. "It's me job."

What they had become... What had they become? Kitty was a whore. Porky was worse, to his way of thinking — but he did it all for her, to keep her safe while she worked. Toffs and such gentleman players called it the "go between." At least that's what it was called in the more polite circles. But here in this part of London it was called by a more common name, "procuring," or just plain "pimping."

"So what did he say?" Kitty asked eagerly. She was sitting in front of the mirror arranging her long auburn hair. It was lustrous, wavy, and she set it in such a way by using ointments and pins so as to cover that part of her face and body so the disfigurement was not easily visible.

"He says he fancies you," Johnson said bluntly.

"Go on!"

"Yes, really, and he told me he will pay good coin to have a go with you tonight."

"How much?" Kitty asked, ever the cunning businesswoman.

"Five quid, paid in gold."

"Go on! Five pounds?"

"In Sovereigns too, not paper bank notes," he said, knowing the knowledge of solid gold coin would bring a smile to her face, making her feel wanted and useful again.

"Well, then… " She smiled, giving him a mock curtsy, "I'm enchanted. So, Porky, where's the dosh?"

Johnson nodded and reached into his coat pocket to hold out five gleaming gold Sovereigns. The coins jingled in his hands with a hypnotizing glare as he showed her the bright gold. "Paid in advance, he did. So I took it right away before he changed his mind. Here it is."

Porky handed the coins to Kitty who took them readily and held them in her hands, looking at each of them, one by one, with joy. Kitty's face was glowing. Each coin showed a gleaming bust of the Queen, Victoria, upon it.

"Blimey," she muttered. "Gold. See how it twinkles in the light."

"Yes," Johnson replied happily. He watched Kitty put the bite on each of the coins, clamping down her teeth on the soft metal to be sure each one was authentic. Soft as only true gold can be, they were. "I told him to pay in advance and he was agreeable, so all is on the up and up. Put them away and keep them safe, dearie. Some of these johns like to take off a poor working gal once the deed is done by not paying afterwards. That'll not happen this time, Kitty. Pay in advance, or no fun tonight, I told 'im!"

"Thank you, Porky. I don't know what I'd do without you."

He smiled, then got down to business, "So let's go now, get it over with, eh? I'll escort you. Best to be on time when serving the quality."

"That's the spirit, Porky. I'll do me job and then we'll split a few pints afterwards, if you're agreeable," Kitty said softly as she took his arm and he took hers. "And who knows, maybe later tonight after the deed is done, you might even get lucky yourself."

"Ah, Kitty, dearie," he said softly. "I always been lucky, ever since I met you."

"Oh, go on now! You say the silliest things sometimes, Porky!" Kitty laughed with a wan smile, but her escort never said a word when he noticed her secretly wipe a lone tear that suddenly ran down her face.

Chapter 2:
Baker Street. 1905

"Busy, busy, busy, Watson! I am nothing, if not a busy bee these days!"

"I see that," my friend the good doctor replied, for he had taken note of my recent flurry of activity.

"This is a momentous time for crime in London. I find myself engaged in no less than three intriguing cases at this very moment," I told him allowing a wry grin as I looked over a group of papers that had lately been brought to me by special messenger.

"So you are in your glory," Watson remarked, noting my good humor. "It is a boon to my soul to see you so focused and engaged after that recent period of inactivity."

"Aye, those dull periods of ennui and doldrums often cause me consternation and even despair. I admit, sometimes I am prone to enter into unhealthy moods of dark depression because of it — sometimes only assuaged by the cocaine needle or the opium pipe."

"Well I am happy to see that such is not the case now."

"Absolutely not, my good man! I find myself completely energized by these current cases."

"Well, would you care to discuss them with me?"

"Only superficially at the moment," I blurted, in the usual rapid staccato voice I employed when finding myself hot upon a case or excited by the discovery of some new evidence that turned a fact upon it's head. "The inventory is really quite interesting. There's that mysterious break-in in Hempstead last weekend where absolutely nothing was stolen. I tell you in all candor, it has me intrigued. Indeed, something very valuable was most certainly stolen."

"I see. What was it?"

"Ah, yes, well, I am afraid I can not say at this time," I replied with a sly grin as Watson sighed openly in disappointment. I could see he was upset that I was being less than forthcoming on the matter, but that would only be for the moment. He well knew my methods and thankfully did not press me for an answer just then. He knew it would come in its own good time.

"Well, it sounds complex," Watson prompted.

"It certainly is. And that is only the one case. Then there is that business of the murder in Kent a fortnight ago of wealthy Charlotte Boothe. I'm afraid her dementia caused her to be locked away by her family for her own protection in a special room with no entrance, or exit, save one. Yet someone, I dare say, passed the alert night nurse stationed outside her door, entered that room, and murdered her. Nevertheless, there are absolutely no indications the room had ever been entered by anyone but her nurse, who is a person above suspicion."

"So the police are baffled?"

"Hah! The police are always baffled."

"Well, I can see that you are entirely in your depth now and enjoying things immensely."

I nodded and smiled full of energy, "Yes that is true. But I have saved the best for last, old fellow. That is the theft of young Billy Somerset's prize bulldog, Pug, which if I do say so, may topple one of England's most influential families from the peerage. I am on my way now to meet with young Billy and plan to examine the Somerset home. So you see, Watson, my plate, as they say, is certainly full at the moment and it do runneth over with examples of our nation's criminous exuberance."

"And what of Lestrade's note?" Watson asked me.

The note had been received by me an hour before. I had opened it immediately, of course, yet had not commented upon it as yet.

I shrugged. "The man has an overactive imagination. He is always getting himself into a pickle of one type or another and expecting me to get him out of it. This time, I believe, I shall pass."

"Pass, Holmes?" Watson's surprise was very openly displayed. It did not shock me, but it gave me pause for I knew he desired further explanation.

"Well, I'm much too busy for Lestrade and his prostitute murder."

"Are you sure, Holmes?"

I laughed indulgently at my friend's concern, "Ah, good Watson, believe me, while it is a rather bloody situation, to be sure, it is after all, just a simple murder. That is all. Nothing out of the ordinary for that part of town."

"But it is murder, Holmes!"

"Yes, and there are twenty such events in and around the London environs every day and night. What would you have me do, go out and solve them all? Is that not what Lestrade and his constables are being paid for?" I looked over at him and saw deep disappointment written large upon his face. To see his hangdog look touched me rather unexpectedly. Well, that was my friend, John Watson. He was such an all-around decent chap. Watson would save the entire world if he could do so, and surely everyone in it. However, I for my own devices, was much more…shall we say…realistic. "I am not being purposefully cold, my friend, nor heartless. Just practical. Sadly, I can not involve myself in every crime and mystery that occurs in and around our fair city. I must choose them carefully."

Watson nodded, "I understand of course, still and all, Lestrade will be disappointed, I imagine."

"I am sure he will be, but he will get over it. Watson, this agency stands firmly upon certain immoveable principles and foundations. The simple truth is that our resources — time and attention — are severely limited. We can not attend to every criminal case in London. No, this murder is not outside the realm of Lestrade's capacity, so he shall just have to put his mind to it and solve it himself."

The doctor sighed, "I imagine you are right."

"Come now, Watson, we are much too busy to indulge such frivolities. Are you with me?"

"You know that I am, Holmes."

"Excellent! Then gather your coat and hat. We leave immediately for Somerset."

"Right now?"

"Yes, Watson, right now. The game is afoot!"

In a heartbeat I took up my coat and rushed down the stairs of our Baker Street lodgings as if the very hounds of hell were after me. Watson ran behind me having grabbed his coat and hat in hand trying to keep up, trying to put on both before we reached the door at the bottom of the stairs. Once there, we ran into our faithful landlady, Mrs. Hudson, who had just opened the front door to let in a very dour and haggard Inspector Lestrade of Scotland Yard.

"Ah, Lestrade," I greeted him cheerily enough, even as he vainly tried to maneuver his bulk into the doorway to block me from leaving. "So glad to see you. Watson and I were just on our way out."

"Holmes!" Lestrade asked sharply, "No, please wait!"

"I am sorry, Lestrade," I told him simply, hoping that would end the matter. Then with a look to my companion I added, "Come now, Watson, we have much work to do today."

Lestrade grabbed my arm and held me back most forcefully with a mighty grasp, "I beg of you, Mr. Holmes. I need you."

Watson and I were both taken aback by the inspector's rash action. I could see my friend grow alarmed once he noted the brief flash of red anger that burst into my face at the affront of being physically held back by Lestrade in such a fashion — but I allowed my anger to subside into a watchful leer.

"Please release me," I said softly, but quite forcefully to the Inspector.

"Of course, Mr. Holmes, I apologize for being overzealous," Lestrade replied quickly releasing my arm. Then he added confidentially, "Please, I need your advice upon a very serious matter."

"Oh, very well, Lestrade," I said reluctantly, seeing as how the Inspector was obviously flustered by some dire problem and found himself in over his head as was too often the case in our long association. I swear, while the fellow possessed many of the worthy attributes of a successful detective, such as a tenacious bulldog nature that allowed him to hunt down criminals, he lacked any measure of the ability to meld facts with imagination to solve a crime. He was entirely in his depth on most common and circumstantial problems but should anything out of the ordinary rear its ugly head, poor Lestrade could often be found floundering on the shores of obtuse confusion. Sighing heavily for the utmost effect, I told him, "Come upstairs and tell me all about it."

"Thank you, Mr. Holmes."

"Think nothing of it," I replied rather unconvincingly.

Once upstairs in our sitting room Watson set down the coat and hat he had never yet had the opportunity to put on; then he motioned Lestrade to a seat. I made myself comfortable in my usual chair as I waited upon what the inspector had to tell me. My eyes examined the man intently. He was frenzied and certainly at loose ends, that much was clear. Something had evidently unnerved the poor fellow.

Watson took the inspector's coat and hat and saw that he was seated comfortably.

I watched our guest intently holding my impatience in check for the moment, "Pray tell, Lestrade, what is on your mind? Something new has come up, no doubt, but please do not tell me that it is that Ripper fantasy that was written about in your note of earlier today. At least I hope it is not."

Inspector Lestrade took a deep breath, nervous tension tinged with fear overcame his features. He was obviously quite troubled by something he had recently seen and he was at a loss on how to begin to tell me about it.

I leaned forward in my chair now much more interested. I am sure good Watson would describe the effect in one of his chronicles for the popular magazines by describing to his readers that I appeared as if I were some frenzied bloodhound smelling hot bait, which after having taken up the scent was all rapt attention and ready to be set lose. Perhaps he would even be correct.

"Here, have a sip of this," good old Watson said, offering the Inspector a small glass of brandy.

Lestrade, usually the serious teetotaler detective never touched spirits while on duty, but now he drank the amber liquid quickly in one gulp. "Thank you, Doctor."

I remained quiet but focused, watching the man intently, eager to hear his news but allowing myself to remain patient for the moment. Lestrade finally shook his head as if coming out of a trance. I could see that Watson couldn't help but wonder what on Earth had so unnerved this seasoned police detective. I must admit, I was keen to know that myself.

"Mr. Holmes, and you, Doctor Watson," Lestrade began awkwardly, looking longingly from one of us to the other, "I know you believe in evil. You have seen the handiwork. Well, I tell you, I have seen evil myself now. Sheer, brutal, evil of a nature I have only once encountered before. I'm in deep on this one with no way out. I need help."

"Of course," Watson offered magnanimously. "I am sure Holmes will be happy to help you any way he is able."

Well that got me hot and I shot my garrulous friend a stern look of rebuke. Watson realized too late that he had jumped the gun by answering too quickly for me without first hearing any of the facts. I looked sharply at him but said not a word, nevertheless I was sure he could feel my chagrin at his outburst of unrestrained enthusiasm by making an offer on my behalf which was not his to make.

Watson caught my eye, nodded suitably contrite. I could not resist answering him with a slight smile of good fellowship. After all, he had meant well.

"Now, go on, Lestrade," I blurted sharply, growing impatient to hear his story. "The facts, please. Only the facts."

The inspector sighed deeply, "There's been a terrible murder. A young lady. A lady of the streets to be sure, but that is of no consequence to me. What does matter is that I do not know what to make of it. The crime was ghastly in the extreme. The lady had been cut open, eviscerated, Mr. Holmes."

Lestrade was plainly shaken by what he had seen; his face was sweating even in the cool autumn temperatures we had been experiencing in London all that week.

"You have blood on your sleeve, Inspector," Watson offered softly.

"Aye, doctor, and blood is not the half if it."

My eyes examined Lestrade carefully but I continued to sit silent, immovable like the statue good Watson often said I appeared to be. At times like these in his little stories of my cases he would avidly describe me as starring off into what he would call some nether realm of time and space not connected with the here and now. Or some such twaddle! Not so, I tell you. Good Watson was often overly dramatic in his descriptions of my so-called powers. I was merely in deep thought. I do get like that sometimes. I did not venture one word yet, but noted the Inspector's bearing and demeanor. That told me all I needed to know, it meant that something grievous was afoot.

Watson took up the gauntlet and said softly, "Inspector, please go on."

"Well...well...I mean...it was simply horrible. More than one of my men lost their breakfast over the sight, let me tell you," Lestrade continued, evidently trying hard to control his emotions. "I'd never seen the likes before, and let me remind you I was in on some of that Ripper business many years ago back in '88. As a young constable I saw what Saucy Jack did to one of the women he played with. What I have seen here now, well... I tell you in all candor gentlemen; it could be by the very same hand. I fear, Mr. Holmes, Jack the Ripper is back!"

"God help us!" Watson stammered, unable to hide his alarm.

There was a moment of stark quiet, then I could bear it no longer, I could not hold back my laughter.

"Holmes!" Watson reacted sharply, as I had foreseen that he would.

"Come now!" I stated sharply to both men, shaking my head with stern disagreement looking squarely at the inspector. "I tell you Lestrade, it

simply can not be."

I am afraid the inspector got quite carried away in his reaction to my words. He looked over at me and showed fear and then utter surprise that I was not buying his theory for one moment.

"Lestrade, Lestrade," I told him rather tartly, shaking my head back and forth as with an errant child, showing my evident amusement. "This is entirely the wrong tact to take in such a problem."

I held my pipe in my hand but did not even bother to light it. Obviously this was some skewed theory by the Inspector brought about by emotionalism and panic, accompanied by not one shred of conclusive evidence. A terrible murder may have been committed, but it in no way could be done by Jack the Ripper. The Inspector's statement was not even up to the magnitude of a one-pipe problem in my estimation.

I saw Watson sigh nervously. I looked at him with a wry grin, he seemed to be seriously considering Lestrade's words, and it was evidently going to be a long day.

"That Ripper business is best left forgotten, Lestrade," I began sharply, trying to impress upon him the need for reality versus fantasy now. "It will only lead you down a blind alley without satisfaction. Women of the night are always getting themselves into trouble; it is a natural hazard of their profession, yet a brutal fact. The fact that in this case a nastier bit of violence has been incorporated into the mix is surely unfortunate, but not altogether unexpected. It does you ill to go off half-cocked — as our American friends are so fond of saying — with your wild Ripper theory. If word of this ever gets out it will panic the city and that ill behooves Scotland Yard. Not good for the career, I'll warrant, either. I'd drop the Ripper theory. You must go to the facts first, before you jump to any theory."

Lestrade sat silently, thinking through what I had told him. He finally shook his head as if dismissing what he'd heard. "You are a wise man, Mr. Holmes and I am sure you are correct in most things, but I feel I must firmly stand my ground on this and go wherever my feelings lead me. You were not there. You did not see what I saw. I tell you something evil is lurking in my city; I have seen its handiwork. I stand by my Ripper theory."

"Really, Lestrade?" I answered sharply, allowing more than a hint of sarcasm to escape my voice now. "It surely is as simple as I say. The hazards of the profession. Were my schedule free, I would be more than happy to assist, I assure you. However, I am afraid I find myself much occupied at the moment with rather more serious cases that also offer me those intriguing aspects I so covet. I am sorry to tell you that I am unable to help

you with — what is after all — a rather pedestrian murder."

"But Mr. Holmes," Lestrade pleaded, his hangdog expression perhaps effective coming from a child but not from a grown Scotland Yard Inspector. It was most unseemly and Watson and I felt some embarrassment for him. He was a good man and a proud one and it saddened me to see him so disabuse himself in such a manner.

I knew for Watson to see Lestrade suddenly so despondent was difficult for the good doctor to take. John was such a decent chap he could not help but take pity upon the inspector, so I could see plainly what was forthcoming.

"Holmes?" Watson asked me, somewhat sheepishly. "Perhaps you could advise the Inspector on some of the finer points? A few hints on where he should focus his efforts. Surely that could do no harm?"

I was silent for a moment, then sighed with defeat "Oh, very well, Watson. Let me tell you, Lestrade, this is, after all, quite simple. A woman of the streets is slain. So you should look in all the usual places that you would in such a case."

"I know, Mr. Holmes, but this all seems rather more serious than the standard street tart killing."

"Every murder is serious, but you do not begin an investigation at the end working backwards — arriving at a theory, no matter how seductive — without sifting through the evidence. You must first work from the evidence and facts only — then go where they lead you," I instructed him. I shook my head sadly. He surely should have known better, and obviously he did, but the man had been severely traumatized by something he had seen. The murder scene had quite obviously unnerved him. I must admit his reaction now really began to interest me, but before anything else, I knew I had to set him firmly on the right course.

"You have made your conclusion on the most superficial appearance of the crime — a rather bloody murder to be sure — but one done merely in the Ripper *style*. Forget this theory for now, it will lead you wrong. Look only at the facts first, then go where they lead you. Only then can you discover the truth."

"I thought I had done just that, Mr. Holmes. Now what?" the Inspector asked reluctantly, obviously embarrassed at his need for help on the case.

"It is plain to me you have been very much shaken by what you have seen, Inspector. The sheer brutality of the murder has shocked you to your very core. I can see that readily. However, you must not allow the emotions of the moment to get in the way of your critical thinking," I told him

this little realizing how those words would come back to haunt me in the coming days. I could see that Lestrade was completely lost at sea here. I did not desire to scold him with disdain but I could not hold back my annoyance that he had come to such a ridiculous conclusion — that of all things the slaying was the result of some new Jack the Ripper — without first following evidence and facts in the proper order.

"Holmes?" Watson prompted softly and I noticed a glint of hope alight in the Inspector's drab face.

"Oh, very well," I sighed once more, allowing my exasperation full reign. "Must I draw you a picture, Lestrade? Well then, look to your suspects in the following order:

Number 1: the husband, if there be one. There may, in fact, be several, official and unofficial.
Number 2: the ex-husband, if there be one, there may be one or more.
Number 3: the boy friend, or more than likely boy friends. This could keep a brace of Bobbies busy for a fortnight.
Number 4: look at any employer — in this case her pimp, who may also function as one of the above.
Number 5: Some tout or tough who hangs around the pubs where she makes her liaisons.
Number 6: a neighbor — some local who lurks about seeking her favor.
Number 7: an unhappy customer, perhaps the last person to see her alive...

Lestrade's face brightened, "I'll see to it at once."

"I am sure that shall keep you and the Yard busy for many a day," I told him rather coldly.

"Well, Holmes," Watson stated with a smile, "I must say, I am simply amazed. In one brief moment you have most logically and succinctly set down a literal and detailed map for the Inspector to follow to catch the culprit and solve the killing."

I acknowledged Watson's remarks with a slight nod. While the good doctor often mentioned how amazed he was by my deductions, in truth of fact it was *I* who was the one who was more often amazed. I was *amazed* that he — as well as so many others — *never* contemplated such obvious deductions in the first place. Oh, well, it was as I have always said, most people see, but they do not truly observe.

"I am sure, Lestrade, that if you look to these topics in the order in which I have given them to you, you will have your man soon enough. I mean, after all, you don't need me for every little murder, do you?" I said unable to hold back one last stinging barb.

Lestrade swallowed hard, "Perhaps you are right, Mr. Holmes. Hazards of the profession, more than likely. Still and all, what was done to that poor woman; the cutting, even the disemboweling was bad enough and quite hard to take in. It was pure evil, sir. However, the pouring of the vitriol upon her face was unseemly and so unnecessary — a truly excessive touch to a ghastly crime."

I suddenly shot up, my eyes grown large in rapt attention now. Had I heard the Inspector correctly? I looked sharply at Lestrade. "Did you say, *vitriol?*"

"Why, yes," Lestrade answered casually. "Vitriol. It is a form of sulfuric acid, I am told."

I felt a cold chill grab me, like the touch of the very hand of Death itself. I grew silent for a long moment, my mind full of dark and brooding thoughts. My eyes seemed to pulse with rage my mind afflux as I thought back to events three years in the past.

Watson looked at me with great concern then, for he could see something serious was afoot. I could not speak for the moment...thinking...asking myself... Could it be?

"Holmes?" Watson asked me carefully. "Holmes, what is it?"

I was silent for a long moment thinking it all through so very carefully. Was it possible? Could it be? Yes, I had to admit, it was most definitely possible! I now realized what may have begun as a situation not even rising to the level of a one-pipe problem may have suddenly gone very far beyond that. Very far indeed!

"Watson, we must drop everything immediately!" I blurted with grim determination. Then to the Inspector, with fire in my voice, I told him, "Lestrade, I will begin work on this case right this instant. I am yours until the end. Lead the way!"

*"Did you say, **vitriol**?"*

Chapter 3:
The Murder Scene

estrade lead the way to a hansom cab that quickly took Watson and me into a deep and drab nefarious section off London's Whitechapel district. This was a drab area packed with the poor and worse whose squalid ambitions and lost hope forced them to live lives of rum-soaked desperation and criminality. The small run-down row houses were merely animal dens rented by poor foreign immigrants at usury rates. It was a grim area where the refuse of empire came to slake their thirsts for easy women, cheap alcohol and the dark dreams offered by the opium pipe.

Of course I was well versed with the area, having entered this section of the city on numerous occasions, but not so for poor Watson. His medical practice did not take him into these dark and dangerous environs. I could only smile when he commented that I seemed to evidence a unique and rather unhealthy knowledge of the area and its people.

Truth be told, I was clearly in my element here, within the stark belly of the criminal cauldron of London, so to speak. It was exciting, even intoxicating for me. Not so, for my long-suffering companion. Nevertheless, I was in my glory here, going so far as to point out various locations of criminal interest — all dubious establishments that had been the scenes of horrendous murders and other terrible acts — to Inspector Lestrade. Of course he was aware of much of what went on here as well, so our conversation grew full of detailed descriptions of the most gruesome violence and dismemberments. This went on for some time and I fear it had grown into a dire criminal catalog that good Watson was loath to hear about. It only ended once our cab pulled up to a stop at a corner building and Watson seemed to be thankful of the fact.

Here we came upon a street where each hovel was a mere shamble.

However at the door of one of these loathsome dens stood a stout London Bobby, standing guard. We exited the cab and Lestrade lead the way to Number 111 and to his man.

"All right now, Jenkins," Lestrade ordered his constable. "Mr. Holmes and Doctor Watson are here to look over the murder scene. No one has been inside since we found her this morning, correct?"

Constable Jenkins stood at rigid attention, "No sir, been sealed tight as a drum since you left. Just as you ordered. No one has been in or out."

"That's the lad," Lestrade said with a nod. "Come now, Mr. Holmes, Doctor, but hold tight to your insides, I warn you."

We entered the dark hovel carefully. The place was a shambles. The odor of dire death hung in the air. There were flies everywhere. Legions of them. The smell was appalling, a mixture of sweat and human waste, with much blood certainly spilled, but there was something else there too. Something vile. The very essence of evil itself or the smell of evil, if such can be said to have a distinctive odor. I have encountered it before, and let me tell you, once you encounter that essence; it never leaves your memory.

The place was nothing more than a front room off the street with a bed in the back. What the more common folk called a "crib," being a place to be used for hourly assignations of the more casual sexual nature which were always paid for in cash beforehand. I remember to this day that evil odor, the buzzing of hordes of flies and the strong coppery smell of blood which seemed to have become aerated so that the place was thick with the fetid taste of it in our mouths as we breathed with great reluctance.

Watson coughed, tightly placing a handkerchief over his nose and mouth.

I looked over at him. "You all right?"

"It is dastardly, the devil himself has done this, Holmes."

I nodded, as I looked around the room.

Lestrade had lit a match and set himself to lighting three lamps that surrounded a bed set flush against the far wall. He eventually illuminated the room well enough so that Watson and I could clearly make out the scene upon the bed. It was absolutely horrific. I could well acknowledge the effect it had upon poor Lestrade coming upon it as he must have, so unawares.

I said not a word but I could feel the faintest twitch on my face below my right eye. It was all nervous anticipation, but I began to wonder just what Lestrade had stumbled on here. While I showed my usual stoic reaction, I tell you dear reader that I was not unaffected by the sheer brutality of the crime. And something more. I had the strange feeling that I knew the victim!

I saw Watson look upon the remains more closely and with a sudden chill I could see that he too recognized something familiar about the woman — though there was God awful left of her for us to see. I can only put it down to some instinct, some slim hint, or insignificant detail that spoke out to me.

Then again, perhaps it was just the hair? Thick auburn, fire red tresses, and I sighed suddenly when I realized that it could be no other than a woman I knew only too well. That meant all my fears about this bestial murder had indeed come true.

Watson cringed, stepping back, for even with all his years as a solid medical man and surgeon, I could see him fight to hold down the bile that was making its way up his throat.

"A right terrible mess, she is, Mr. Holmes," Lestrade offered grimly. "I can not get the image out of my mind. It is disturbing in the extreme."

"It was meant to be. It is a message."

"A message, Mr. Holmes. But to whom?"

To me. But I said nothing. I advanced carefully, examining the room, the bed and its environs minutely. I took out my magnifying glass and used it to closely examine the blood spots on the bed clothes, the floor and upon a space rug in front of the bed. I looked for directionality, paying particular attention to the tails of the blood spots that always indicate how the murder was committed. It was not a pretty sight. The walls had blood sprayed everywhere, but there was valuable information to be gleaned there as well which I collected and stored away for later use. Finally I visually examined the body — or what was left of it — touching nothing for the moment, but taking particular note of the location, position and the disfigurement done to the corpse.

"Just as we found her, Mr. Holmes," Lestrade offered.

I nodded and continued my investigation.

While I looked over the scene, Constable Jenkins entered the room and called Lestrade to a brief conference by the doorway. The two men spoke in soft whispers for some minutes. Watson stood at my side, aghast by what lay in that bed before us as he watched me intently.

"God, who could so such a thing?" he asked.

Ignoring his question for the moment I asked, "So, Watson, what do you make of it?"

The doctor shook his head sadly. He moved forward to perform his examination of what was left of the woman's upper torso. "She was butchered, cut open with a long blade, perhaps a butcher knife of some kind or a military bayonet; and Holmes, this was done while she was still alive. There is not much left to make any identity, it appears that her face has been eaten away with some manner of acid."

I nodded; still busy with my looking glass, tweezers, and a small glass vial I had on hand to collect evidence.

"This is beastly, Watson, and utterly underserved," I muttered harshly, allowing my anger to show on this rare occasion. "Vitriol has been used. Just as it had been used once before. Do you remember? I fear it has now become his calling card. I promise you, he shall pay for this!"

"He?" Watson asked curious.

"Why, it can be none other than Baron Adelbert Gruner." I replied simply. "I am sure you remember the name and the many crimes associated with it?"

"I most certainly do remember him, Holmes. He is a man I could hardly ever forget. But you think he is responsible for this?"

Three years back Gruner had tried to have me murdered by street toughs. Then he attempted to prosecute Watson and me for the burglary of his home and the theft of a certain unsavory book that ended his ambitions of a lofty marriage to a noble lady, and by doing so we served a most illustrious client.

"This has all his hallmarks," I said softly.

"Are you sure, Holmes?"

"Undoubtedly."

Watson was silent for a moment, his eyes upon the remains before us.

"This then must be...?"

"Yes, it is Kitty Winter."

Watson looked at the figure upon the bed as if seeing her for the first time now; a great sadness overcame his features, now that he was sure of her identity. It was always worse when the corpse was a person known to us.

"Does Lestrade know who she is?"

"I think not. I shall alert him to her identity in a moment."

Watson stood by me as I bent to view the corpse from every possible angle, still without moving the body. The vitriol had eaten away most of the skin of Kitty's face and damaged much of the upper torso, making her seemingly unidentifiable, leaving behind a melted mass of raw flesh. It was ghastly and so unnecessary, but for the one salient fact that all this had been done to send a message to me.

"Vitriol, Watson. Only one man uses vitriol on women and that is Gruner."

Lestrade came back to us now from his meeting with Constable Jenkins, who had left the room to resume his post.

"Good news, Mr. Holmes, you are apparently correct. It is not a new Jack the Ripper after all, merely a spurned lover, as you suggested. I am relieved to admit that I was wrong about this being the work of another Ripper. We have found the killer. He is being held at Scotland Yard at this very moment."

My eyes darted upwards at that news, "Excellent, Lestrade. So who is the man?"

"Therein lies the rub, as yet we are unable to identify him. He will not speak to my men or even give his name, but he's a local lout by the looks of him, so it won't take my boys long to identify him." Lestrade said proudly. "I'm sure we have some record on him, we always do with his kind. We found him with blood on his hands, so there can be little doubt as to his guilt. As you told me, a simple case, probably some boyfriend, pimp, or combination of the two, as is usually the case."

"Can you identify the victim?" Holmes asked the Inspector.

"Not likely with all that mess there, but I will have the body sent to the morgue for closer examination and an autopsy. They may come up with something useful. No papers or any other means of identification were found upon the body or within the room. There was no purse or handbag found. That room was rented by the hour by a man who left no name, as is so often the case in these sordid assignations. However, I am sure that once we get the man held at the Yard to talk, he'll give up all the particulars we need."

I offered a wry grin, "Well, Lestrade, I really must congratulate you. I see that you have everything well in hand. You have come a long way since this morning," I said with a wry grin, seeing the Inspector preen himself at my words of encouragement, even though they had been uttered by me with grim humor behind them and in considerable jest.

I saw Watson give me a knowing smile.

I turned back to the inspector and added, "However, there is one fact I can add that you do need to know, Lestrade. The woman's name. It is Kitty Winter. She was involved in the Baron Gruner case three years back. You may remember her case? She had been wronged by the Baron and disfigured by him. In revenge she threw a bottle of vitriol into his face which disfigured the man for life. She spent two years in prison for the offense. However, the circumstances of her crime were so unique her incarceration was of minimal duration. She has been out of prison for the last six months plying her trade in London's East End and here in Whitechapel."

Lestrade nodded slowly, "Yes, I remember the case, Mr. Holmes. I also seem to remember that you and the doctor went quite a bit over the line on that one. Charges of burglary, was it not?"

"False charges, never proved," Watson came forward in explanation.

I cleared my throat in feigned exasperation, "I think you will find the man you are holding is Baron Gruner, for he has motive for revenge against Miss Winter."

"Well then, could you help me with one more tiny thing?" Lestrade asked more contrite. "The man we are holding will not talk, but he has told us that he will readily speak to — Sherlock Holmes."

"Really? Very well then, Lestrade, lead the way. It appears we must hear what this man has to tell us."

Chapter 4:
Scotland Yard

I am afraid good old Watson had not often been to the "Yard," as it was simply called back then by most people. No, he had not been there in quite a few years and never to the new building. That imposing new granite edifice stood proudly as a monument to stout British law enforcement and was a bastion against crime. I, of course, knew the building intimately, though I never suspected at the time that I would soon know it even more intimately and in a manner I could never imagine.

Inspector Lestrade lead us into the building and then down into the lower depths where the jail cells were located. The noise and odor down there were assaulting to the senses and the place was stark and fearfully intimidating to someone of the gentry, such as poor old Watson.

"How can these criminals deal with this grim atmosphere, being locked away in such a small iron-barred cell all hours of the day and night, and for God knows what ghastly crimes?" Watson asked obviously appalled by the place and the nefarious people locked away within.

Lestrade replied, "It does not seem to bother them that much. Most accept their plight with a stoic realism once they are caught, though I am sure each and every one of them would do anything within their power to seek release and taste sweet freedom again. Of course, they all proclaim their innocence with the righteous indignation of the local vicar discovered in a Cheapside knocking shop."

Watson shrugged sadly, "Still and all, it must be terrible to be locked away here."

"Actually, the national prisons are far worse, old man, believe me," I told Watson confidently as we walked down the stark corridors. "The men of Scotland Yard adhere to a high standard of professionalism in everything they do. Or at least they try to do so. We might wish these standards existed throughout the entire British penal system."

Lestrade nodded proudly, as he escorted us into another corridor where I noticed one stout fellow come close to the bars of his cell and stare at me intently.

Suddenly the man shouted from between the bars, "What's this! Not the famous Sherlock Holmes?"

As we passed the man's cell I looked at him with a wan smile and answered sharply, "Well now, how are you, Quimby? Are you behaving yourself?"

"Aye, Mr. Holmes, I'm well enough. I'm being the right proper gentleman in here, I am, no choice really," then he laughed harshly and his joke was joined in by all the others locked in the cells around him.

I looked at the fellow and remarked, "Quimby has considerable talent with a knife, Watson. A cutpurse with an ill temper, he sometimes gets carried away and leaves a corpse behind for his troubles. He robbed a man in Regent Park and when the man protested, Quimby slit his throat. Quite cleanly, I might add. I'm afraid this is just the place for Mr. Quimby until the assizes put him away for good — or give him a taste of the rope."

"Aye, he's a bad one," Lestrade commented giving the criminal a harsh get-back stare and leading us down the corridor towards another block of cells.

"Goodbye, Quimby," I said with finality as I walked away from him.

"Goodbye, Mr. Holmes," Quimby's voice receded as we disappeared down the hallway.

"What will happen to him?" Watson asked.

"Scheduled for the hangman's noose, tomorrow morning," Lestrade answered grimly. "British law has little patience with the likes of murderers."

"I see. I imagine it is nothing more than he deserves, after all," Watson replied, then he drew his attention to the reason we were there. "So what of this new fellow you have in custody, Lestrade?"

"You'll see him soon enough. He's being held in the Special Wing, which is for high security prisoners, down the hall and just past these locked doors."

There was a constable on duty at the doorway and upon Lestrade's order he unlocked the stout iron door that opened into another corridor — the Special Wing. Here we were led into a much shorter corridor with cells on both sides, but almost all appeared empty. It was much quieter here also.

Watson and I followed behind Lestrade as he kept a brisk pace. I kept up easily for I was certainly anxious to get to that cell and see the man Lestrade had held there. Our footsteps echoed down the hall as we approached the end of the corridor. There we saw a man in another iron-barred cell, a stout man sitting upon a cot. The man looked up at us as we approached, but as yet had said nothing.

Of course I was expecting to see Baron Aldebert Gruner, what I saw was...

"Shinwell 'Porky' Johnson?" I asked completely surprised to see the fellow again — and to find him here in a Scotland Yard jail cell.

The man looked up and stared at me closely, then suddenly recognized me.

"What on earth are you doing in here?" I asked the man, and even moreso I wondered, where was Gruner?

"Good to see you again, Mr. 'Olmes," the man stood up now, a broad grin upon his big lumpy face. It was obvious he'd taken a recent beating but he was not the type to complain. "So good to see you again, sir. And the Doctor is here, too."

"Where is Baron Gruner?" I asked Lestrade, so surprised and annoyed by this obvious mistake on his part that I had to hold my temper in check.

"Baron Gruner? I don't know what you mean. This is the man who murdered the woman," Lestrade said simply. "It is all plain and clear now, Mr. Holmes."

I was appalled, looking at the inspector with my mouth actually agape, totally shocked by what had happened as my temper seethed silently. Nevertheless I held things in check; I nodded thoughtfully, leaving things for the moment as I took a closer look at the man in the cell before me.

I was alarmed to note the man's injuries and looked to Lestrade who simply shrugged unknowingly. Then I spoke to the prisoner, "And those lumps? Did you get them from the Bobbies?

"No, Mr. 'Olmes. I've been treated well enough here by the peelers. I can not complain."

"Of course, I remember you too now!" Watson blurted looking from the prisoner and then back to me. "This is the man you sent out to find Miss Winter during the de Meriville marriage case."

"Quite right, Watson."

"Mr. Johnson, is it not?" Watson asked.

"Yes, I be Shinwell Johnson, who most call Porky. It be good to see you again, Doctor," the prisoner replied.

"What have they done to you, Porky?" I asked vastly concerned to see him in a cell where the Baron should have been.

"Not me, Mr. 'Olmes, they done it to me darling, Kitty," Johnson told us in a hard tone laced with severe pain and anger. "I tried me best to protect her, I swears it! I told her she didn't have to do that kind of work no more, but you knew her heart and her head better than most. Both were hard, sir, 'cepting where I'm concerned. Now's she's gone. Gone and lost to me forever!"

The man suddenly tore into a torrent of tears that he had obviously held in check until our arrival. We remained quiet and allowed him his time to mourn Kitty.

I decided to engage Lestrade discretely, so we moved away from the cell, "Inspector, this man's name is Shinwell Johnson, known on the street as Porky, a career criminal, cutpurse and cutthroat, a very bad fellow and certainly you will find him prominently displayed in your records for all manner of crimes. However, I can assure you that he did not murder Kitty Winter."

"How can you say that? Wasn't he her pimp? Her boyfriend? You told me to seek out just such a man. I did." Lestrade stated tersely, growing annoyed at having to explain every bit of evidence to me. "So here he is. He also was found with blood on his hands. I am certain the blood belongs to the murdered woman. It is being tested now and once I receive the report I am sure we will have a match as to blood type."

"No doubt," I replied, with a dismissive shrug.

"No doubt, Mr. Holmes, that's easy for you to say. Harder to explain, I'll warrant," Lestrade chided.

"There could be a logical reason for the blood," Watson offered with his usual helpfulness.

"Bravo, old man!" I blurted in support of my friend's remark.

Lestrade just gave us a derisive snort.

To the inspector I added, "The man discovered the body because they worked together and she was his lover, there is your explanation for the blood."

Lestrade was not moved, he just shook his head, forever playing the part of the obstinate copper. "He'll not talk to us, so until he does…"

"I'll talk now! I'll tell you all and truthful I will. Now that Mr. 'Olmes is here," Johnson said sternly, drying his tears and making a powerful effort to control his emotions.

Lestrade and I, with Watson alongside, moved closer to the jail bars.

"Very well, Porky. Now tell me all that happened from the very beginning," I asked sternly. "Leave out nothing."

"I shall do my best, Mr. 'Olmes," Johnson told us softly with a sad kind of pride. "Well, me and that gal went back a long ways. Even before you caught me at my thieving trade and had me sent away for a time. I'm not complaining, you understand, I knew I done bad by the law and I deserved what I got."

"I well remember, you were just a young lad back then," I told him.

"Aye, you remember me, but do you remember Kitty? She was a rare, fine beauty in them days, she was. The belle of the city — leastways my part of the city."

"So tell me what happened that day, Porky?"

"It was terrible, sir, she died terrible." Johnson took a deep breath, then fought to continue. "She had a job, she did. A good paying one with a right proper toff. He paid five quid for the use of her for the evening. I didn't want her to go but once she saw the gold, well you knows what they say — the way to a gal's heart is paved with gold. Anyway, that was me Kitty, she was ever one for the dosh. So I took her to Number 111, but I was standing for no foolishness there, so I stood guard outside the room out upon the street, with me club in hand. Just for insurance, ye understand? She didn't want me to be there, of course. She told me my look would scarce her customer away, my brutish face and manners might make him think I was there to give him a drubbing and rob 'im, but I didn't care. We already had the dosh and she was tickled pink about that. She just wanted to earn her money quick and be done with the job. I finally told her I'd go off and leave her be for some private time with her customer, but I lied and stayed close. I did my turn as guard, I did. I watched her go inside. After a short time I heard her laughter, saw the lights go dim…then…"

He stopped for a moment.

"I know it is difficult for you," I said, having some knowledge of their long relationship.

"Aye, you see Kitty was a special lass. I took a fancy to her right away in me own way, Mr. 'Olmes. When I saw what the Baron did to her three years aback… Well, a lot of men saw her as damaged goods after that — she being so disfigured of face and form. I tell you truly, I never noticed it at all. I only saw her as she looked that first time I met her so many years ago, the young lass with a big smile on her face, the sparks in her lovely big eyes, that lustrous long red hair. I tell you, she was a rare and fine beauty in them days, though a gal brought up in rough circumstances. Like we all was in this part of town."

"You loved her?" Watson asked.

Johnson looked at my companion hard, the intensity in his eyes flared, then died down, "Aye, Doctor, I loved her from that first moment I set eyes upon her, to that last moment I seen what that fiend had done to her in that terrible bloody room."

"So tell me now," I continued, "what exactly did you see?"

Johnson took a deep breath, obviously marshalling his thoughts. "It weren't much, I'm afraid. I stood guard over Kitty, ready to bust into the room if I heard the man do her harm. Some men feel they have the right to hurt a woman when they purchase her favors. Let me tell you, I was standing for none of that action with me Kitty."

"Bravo!" Watson blurted with enthusiasm.

I shot my companion a rapid hand gesture indicating he was to be silent, then I nodded towards Johnson for him to continue his story.

"Well," Johnson added, "all was quiet for a while, as these things usually go at first. Then I heard some laughter, then more quiet. It appeared Kitty had things well in hand. I was ready to take my guardianship as usual when I was suddenly set upon by two or three boyos. Proper professionals they were too. Took me down quickly and quite handily."

Johnson looked over at me and shook his head sadly, there was a look of shame on his face now that he had failed his beloved Kitty, and that he had no more to offer than that.

"Please continue."

"Well, Mr. 'Olmes, I must have been out for hours. When I came to I found myself alone in an alley down the street. Once I regained my senses and realized what had happened I immediately feared for Kitty and ran back to Number 111. Like a mad man I burst open the door. There I found her, dead on the bed as you've seen her, her naked body ravaged by deep wounds and cuts, and some kind of acid thrown upon her face as she lay tied down and helpless. I only pray it all was done *after* she had been killed, but… Knowing your Baron's evil ways, Mr. 'Olmes …I fear the worst."

Johnson shed more tears, silent and pain wracked. We all felt for him. The big brute had a soft spot in his heart for Kitty Winter that much was plain to see, and he took no shame in showing it. True love, I realized with evident surprise and awe at the sheer grace of it all; true love exhibiting itself in the very strangest of places and amongst the most unlikely of people.

"Mr. 'Olmes, I did not see the toff who employed her. I only worked with a go-between — as I was — a man who told me his name was Sergey and that he wanted to purchase Kitty's favors for his master who had seen her one day and was keen to have her for himself. I got no last name or address. It was all done on the cuff, like, the way these things are commonly done," Johnson continued giving full vent to his anger now. "So help him if I ever catch him! He'd paid me as a go between. It wasn't the Baron himself, of that I am sure. Perhaps this Sergey is a man working for him? Or some dupe the Baron used. I hear the Baron was terribly scarred from what my Kitty did to him. That is good! Kitty had her revenge, but now the Baron's had his revenge. Now I want me own revenge, Mr. 'Olmes. Get him! Make him pay!"

"And what of Kitty's blood on your hands?" Watson asked softly. "The police consider it to be conclusive evidence of your guilt."

Johnson looked at Watson, nodded, "Aye, doctor, it is Kitty's blood. When I was taken I had her blood on me hands just as the inspector says. When I burst in and found her, I tried me best to revive her, even though I barely knew what to do so severe were her wounds. I knew me efforts would not bring her back but still I tried, and so I got her blood on me hands and on me clothing. It is the only thing I have now that is left of her."

Watson nodded grimly looking at the poor wretch before us. I saw him notice the blood spots still on the man's face and shoulders. Kitty's blood, from where he'd lovingly held her to him in death. It was a sorrowful sight and I was not untouched by it.

"The man is innocent, Lestrade," I said simply. "You must release him. This man could no more kill Kitty Winter that I could kill Doctor Watson here. He was entirely devoted to Kitty."

"I can not release him," the Inspector replied in a severe tone that told me he had become all business and by the rules. "He must remain in gaol, stand trial and then pay for his crime. Unless you can clear him, Mr. Holmes."

"Lestrade, you can trust my word. He is innocent of these charges," I insisted with severe exasperation. "Remember, not one hour ago, you were entirely convinced this murder was done by the Ripper himself!"

"Nevertheless, this man is the killer. I am convinced we have our man. Now it is for the courts to decide. We have the evidence on our side. He was at the murder scene by his own admission. He also has her blood on his person. There is much to recommend him, Mr. Holmes."

"You are making a grave error," I said forcefully. "You also were at the murder scene and as the good doctor pointed out, you also have her blood on your person. Does that make you the killer?"

"The man is innocent, Lestrade. You must release him."

Lestrade allowed a grim smile, "All inconsequentials, I am afraid, Mr. Holmes. Inconsequentials and you know it."

"You are making a grave error, Lestrade."

"I must concur with Holmes," Watson added sharply.

Lestrade remained obstinate; he would hear nothing more on the matter.

As we left Shinwell Johnson's jail cell, Lestrade became standoffish and grew taciturn. I knew there was no moving him without new evidence. I did not speak, nor even argue with the man, so rigid had his position regarding Johnson become. I decided to bide my time. I knew I would need to get Johnson out of his cell, because I wanted his help in tracking down the Baron.

Once back upstairs in Inspector Lestrade's office, I tried for one last time to explain why Johnson was innocent of the charge. I even pled for Johnson's release. Watson joined me in these entreaties, but Lestrade would hear nothing of it. He would not budge from his obstinate and official police position without contradictory evidence. Evidence I did not possess just then.

"The man is innocent, I tell you!" I protested harshly.

"He is a career criminal and you know it!" Lestrade replied, as if that was the last word on the matter. "He was with the woman when she died and he had her blood on his person. He is perfect for the part. I can not in good conscience allow his release, nor recommend bail."

"Well you are very wrong about him. Johnson has been a useful agent, I myself have used him on numerous occasions, and I repeat that he is innocent of this murder."

"Listen to Holmes, he would not steer you wrong," Watson added.

Lestrade finally nodded, "That very well may be, but the evidence tells me otherwise. We work on evidence here, Mr. Holmes, not opinion, as you have so often impressed upon me lately."

I stepped back, stung by the rebuke and the irony.

Faithful Watson was not so easily subdued.

"Opinion!" Watson stammered now in anger, "That is outrageous! What evidence first brought you to the *opinion* that this was the work of the Ripper!"

Lestrade looked grim but said nothing.

I gave the good doctor a wry grin, he had hit the mark splendidly in his usual manner of bluster. I could see Watson was highly insulted by the very use of the word "opinion" by Lestrade. Surely the inspector knew better than that. Watson was visibly upset with the inspector for having the temerity to state that my argument could ever be based upon mere opinion.

I held up a hand to stay his anger. "Call it opinion if you like, Lestrade. But, I know Porky Johnson and I knew Kitty. I know the type of people they are and I know exactly what they are capable of. I know them as well as I know good Watson here."

"Well, then what of this mysterious Sergey, a giant of a man and the go-between, that Johnson mentions?" he asked curtly.

"An Austrian, I'll wager, and certainly one of the Baron's men."

Lestrade shook his head, "Well, what of the young gentleman who hired the girl then? And what of this Sergey? Neither man has been found, and I venture to say no such persons exist."

"Oh, I am sure one will be found soon enough. Sergey is certainly one of the Baron's henchmen and is long gone by now. He'll not be found. However, our young gentleman may yet turn up, if we are lucky. He may be some dupe used to bait the trap, probably some youthful layabout upper-class toff. Inspector, you'll not find Sergey, but I would strongly consider taking note of any missing men from the quality set, as well as recent suspicious deaths of young men in the upper class."

"I shall look into it," Lestrade promised.

I nodded, "Thank you, you may be interested in what you find."

"I said I shall look into it, Mr. Holmes," Lestrade answered in a short clipped tone that seemed to signal the end of the interview.

I nodded curtly, "Well then, it appears we are done here, doctor. Let us be off."

Then Watson and I left Scotland Yard, both of us quietly holding our tempers in check with Lestrade and the machinery of the official police.

Chapter 5
The Case Grows Deeper

Once we left Scotland Yard, Watson and I stopped off for a much needed short lunch. When we returned to Baker Street we were surprised to find a message from Lestrade waiting for us, having been sent by special messenger. I read it and smiled. It was beginning to all come together.

"Aha! See that Watson, it appears Lestrade has found Johnson's toff!" I stated as I handed him the note. "It is none other than young Simon Germain, rakehell and scion of the wealthy Germain family. He has been known for his many dalliances with the ladies — high-brow and low. His body has just been discovered in an alley off Montgomery Street, his throat very neatly slit."

"That is terrible, Holmes!"

"Baron Gruner has taken care of any loose ends," I added as I went for my pipe and tobacco.

Watson watched me as I silently stuffed my pipe, while he poured himself a two-fingered glass of port. This was becoming a thick little problem, seemingly thicker by the moment. I was angry at the murder of Kitty, but also the sheer injustice being done to Shinwell Johnson.

"Watson, as angry as I might have appeared with our inspector friend, this is not Lestrade's fault. Nor the Yard's," I said softly, for I knew the real villain behind this all. "The official police are merely doing their duty as they see it. I'm afraid all that has transpired has been part of Baron

Gruner's plan from the very beginning. It is all his handiwork. Everything that has happened — and more importantly, everything yet to come — will be his doing. I am sorry to admit that I underestimated the man and his deep capacity for revenge."

"How so, Holmes?"

"He took his revenge against Kitty, then neatly set up Porky as the killer," I stated with a deep sigh. "He will not stop there. I am afraid that he will take his revenge against me as well, old boy. If you remember, I played a considerable part in his downfall. I am sure that he shall make another attempt to kill me."

My words had an icy effect upon Watson, but I knew that his fear was not for his own person; so much as it was for mine.

He looked at me deeply, "Can it be true? So then, you are in danger?"

"Very serious danger, my friend."

Watson digested the ominous meaning of my words.

Meanwhile, I paced the room like some nervous bridegroom, puffing on my pipe, swirls of smoke surrounding me, not saying a word. We were in a fix like we had never found ourselves before.

It was bare moments later when Mrs. Hudson informed us that we had a visitor.

"I wonder who that could be?" Watson asked, looking at me for some answer.

I remained silent. I had my hunch. For knowing the deep situation we were now in, I was sure who our visitor might be. It was not long before I heard Mycroft's ponderous weight slowly climbing the stairs as he entered our sitting room. My older brother looked tired and concerned. He gave us a grim smile.

Watson welcomed my brother, took his coat and led him to a seat across from my own. He then handed him a glass of what I was sure my egalitarian brother would consider to be a barely passable brandy. Mycroft was seated on our divan, his corpulent bulk seeming comfortable while his face showed signs of grave concern.

"I heard about the girl, of course. I am sorry, Sherlock," he began softly.

I nodded, "She deserved a better end than that."

I had nothing else to say and kept myself busy by stuffing my favorite pipe full of tobacco and relighting it, but I was not happy being reminded about what had been done to Miss Winter and I admit I was trying to hide my emotions on the matter like I so often do.

"I knew you would not come to see me about this, Sherlock, so I decided that when Mohammed will not go to the mountain, then the mountain must go to Mohammed." Mycroft told me with a slight laugh.

"I am no Mohammed."

"And, I, Sherlock, am no mountain," Mycroft replied, then with a lusty laugh he added, "though I am sure I could stand to lose a stone or two in weight, eh?"

I allowed a wry grimace.

My brother just nodded and took a rather disapproving sip of his brandy.

"So then, what is it? It must be something momentous to rouse you from the secluded environs of your beloved Diogenes club, eh?" I asked all serious now.

"Lestrade has stumbled upon something…unfortunate… It will get you dangerously involved," Mycroft stated simply.

"I am already involved. Watson as well."

Mycroft nodded grimly.

We were all silent for a moment. Then I asked my brother most carefully, "Just answer one question, Mycroft. Does this murder have anything to do with your government work or with any of the doings of the Diogenes Club?"

"Upon my soul, it does not! But there are certain ancillary aspects you need to be made aware of. That is why I am here."

"I see. Then I believe you, Mycroft."

"As you should, Sherlock."

I gave my brother a sly look, "So what now?"

"That girl, it was nasty, nasty business," Mycroft mused sadly.

"He shall pay dearly for that," I replied and I could not help but grit my teeth in a measure of fiery determination I'd rarely allowed before. My blood was up.

"However, there are complications that you need to be made aware of, Sherlock, and you as well, Dr. Watson."

"Yes?" Watson asked carefully. "Such as…"

"I am afraid this is beyond the usual thing that comes up in my brother Sherlock's work, even when dealing with the nobility. Albeit the man is a foreigner," Mycroft continued, taking a sip of his port as though he was a doomed man. It was obvious that he did not relish what he about to tell us.

"Go on," I told my brother.

"Three years ago, through my contacts, I was able to ensure that Baron

Gruner's charges against you and the doctor for burglary of his London home were dismissed. However, the assault charge upon his person by Miss Winter was a far more serious matter that I could not so easily erase. Miss Winter did not fare as well. As you know she had to take almost two years in prison — a not unreasonable term for her manner of crime. It is only because of the extenuating circumstances that she was offered the leeway she received. After the attack on the Baron by Miss Winter, it was reported the man's injuries caused him to return to his native Austria for a long convalescence and lonely reclusion. The damage to him was said to be extensive, even ghastly."

"Kitty Winter received no less from him and for no good reason," I reminded my brother.

I saw Watson nod deeply; he was obviously recalling the intricacies of the case from three years back. It was a case that he had been after me to allow him to write up and publish since it had first occurred. I could not allow that because of the high-born persons involved and the obvious complications, but I told him that perhaps, some years later, I might relent and allow publication. Watson wrote up the case and I allowed publication last year in *The Strand* magazine under his title of "The Adventure of The Illustrious Client." I believe it was one of my most dangerous cases.

It all came back to me now, of course. It had been a horrible affair in so many of its aspects. The handsome and charming Baron Adelbert Gruner had announced his impending marriage to the lovely and wealthy Violet de Merville, the press lauding it as the marriage of the year. But the Baron had a dark side, which contained a vile beastliness of such depths that I had never encountered before. He had murdered his first wife back in Austria, but had never been brought to book for what was eventually termed an "accident." It had been no accident, of that I was certain.

The simple fact is that the man was a monster. He had somehow bewitched the innocent young de Merville woman so that she would hear no ill word against him. The control he held over her seemed complete, even diabolical. Violet's father feared such a marriage, and through an intermediately — Watson's so-called 'Illustrious Client' — who sought my help on the case. Right away I realized that this marriage would mean the woman's certain doom. In the course of my investigation I discovered another previous victim of Baron Gruner's beastliness, his former mistress, the lovely model Kitty Winter. She had been a beautiful young woman whom Gruner had disfigured with vitriol in a ghastly act of revenge and spite when she left him because of his evil ways. She'd seen only too well the man's true nature and was appalled by it.

Now, years later, Miss Winter had been discovered to be the murdered woman whose vicious slaying had so shocked Lestrade. Baron Gruner's revenge, no doubt, for her attack upon him three years previous.

I remember well Kitty's shocking use of the acid upon the Baron back then, three years ago on that fateful night when I had caused Watson to pose as a wealthy collector of rare Chinese porcelain. It was a ruse which gave me the time I needed to burgle the Baron's home. There I obtained the brown leather book that turned the case upon its head. It was a book in which the Baron chronicled all of his vicious evils perpetuated upon the many young and innocent women he had been involved with over the years. It was the book that Kitty told me she had seen once at his home, and that she said should have been titled, *Souls I Have Ruined*. That horrendous vile book, written in the Baron's own hand proved to be the one instrument that collapsed the love of Violet de Merville for him once and for all — and very probably saved the young woman's life as well.

"If Baron Gruner is back," I said simply, "there is great danger."

`"Great danger, indeed," Mycroft warned sternly.

"Have you or your men seen him? Do you know his whereabouts?" Watson asked my brother.

"No, Doctor, there are some hints, rumors only, but nothing definite. Officially he is still back in Austria, recovering from his injuries," Mycroft stated flatly.

Watson nodded, swallowed hard at all that had been said, and the implications of it all. But the good doctor was made of sterner stuff and I could see that he was determined to ride it out with me come what may.

Stout old Watson!

Well of course Watson and I had done it before on numerous occasions and always come through. He knew the Baron to be a violent man. Gruner had once tried to have me murdered in the street by a gang of toughs. Of course that could never be linked back to the Baron. Watson also had been at my side when for many days the London papers reported that I lay near death from that attack. Now Baron Gruner was back in London to finish what he had begun years before.

Mycroft sighed and continued, "Be that as it may, years ago I was able to intervene and have you and the Doctor cleared of charges of burglary at the Baron's home. I made it all go away, as they say. As you know I have some influence at Whitehall, in the Foreign Office. However, Baron

Gruner is a resourceful and powerful Austrian nobleman — I need not remind you that the Austro-Hungarian Empire, and their big brother, the German Empire of the Kaiser, are now at odds with Great Britain. These are delicate times, Sherlock, Doctor, so we must move carefully. I am afraid that were I, or any of my numerous proxies, to be connected to any incident that caused the demise of Baron Gruner, it could result in war. Devastating world war, I am afraid. That is why I am sorry to tell you both, that you will have to handle this situation on your own, without any direct action from me or those connected with the government."

I nodded silently, accepting my brother's grim words on the situation with my usual stoicism. He was, after all, correct; doing his job for King and Empire.

"I assume the enemies of Great Britain are looking for just such a pretext to begin military operations against the Empire?" I asked him.

Mycroft nodded grimly, then took a deep breath, "What I tell you now is secret information, so it should never leave this room. At the Foreign Office we have run many detailed extrapolations on the possibilities of war breaking out in Europe through the various alliances. This is all quite hush-hush stuff and very complex, however there are certain incontrovertible scenarios. The highest probabilities all indicate the worst scenario would occur as the result of the assassination of an Austrian nobleman. It would turn Europe into chaos."

"And Baron Gruner is an Austrian nobleman," I said simply.

"The extrapolations do not mention a specific person, Sherlock, but the implication is clear and the danger is terribly real," my brother added.

Watson shook his head, looking at my bother more astonished than fearful, "Surely, you can do something, Mr. Holmes? Having the man arrested for murder might be a starter. Have him deported. Maybe, even have one of your 'Special Branch' chaps give him a little likewise payback for what he did to poor Kitty Winter?"

"Nothing would give me greater pleasure," Mycroft smiled at Watson patiently. Then he looked over to me, "I see the Doctor is a good friend and a stout hearted passionate chap."

I allowed a slim smile, "There is none truer."

Watson appeared heartened by my words but became dismayed to learn that we would receive no help from the official government.

Finally I explained, "It is no coincidence Baron Gruner is in London now. The reason is because he has chosen to act upon some plan of revenge and we must do all we can to stop him. We must also accept that brother Mycroft's hands are tied. What would you have him do? Assassinate Gruner? That could precipitate a war between the British Empire and Austria-Hungry — along with their Germanic allies. Gruner has close familial ties to the Hapsburgs. Such an act could mean world war, Watson. A devastating world war. The very thing we have feared and tried to stave off in Europe ever since the days of Napoleon. It must not be allowed to happen again. In any case, we can not locate the Baron, so any such action now is purely moot. No, you and I must work this out on our own, old friend."

"I see," he sighed, looking deflated.

"Buck up, old man, we shall persevere as we always have," I told him, relieved to see my words bring the hint of a smile to his face.

"The least I can do is loan you some of my men, undercover and quite unofficially of course, to seal off Baker Street and hopefully make 221B a fortress that Baron Gruner's men can not enter," my brother told us.

"Thank you, Mycroft," I said, "if not for me, then at least for poor Watson's benefit."

I am afraid that Watson bristled at that statement.

"I am fully capable of defending myself in any situation!"

"Of course you are, Doctor," Mycroft said, allowing a wry grin.

"Think nothing of it, old chap, it was a callous remark on my part and I apologize. It is just that I want you to understand that if the Baron seeks to get at me, there is little that Mycroft's men, or anyone else, may be able to do to stop him."

Watson looked at me and my brother carefully, "It is just that I was never aware you were in such imminent peril. What of the official police? Scotland Yard should surely be alerted."

"I'm afraid our old friend Lestrade is in charge," I reminded him.

"Hah, not him, not the little ferret?" Mycroft commented with a snicker.

"The same," I responded. "He has already made an arrest in the Winter murder."

"Let me guess? The wrong man?"

"Naturally," I stated and there seemed nothing more to say upon the matter.

Mycroft and I looked at each other knowingly. He looked intent, serious, but soon I saw a softness enter his gaze and could see the affection and concern he held there for me. And for Doctor Watson. I was truly touched.

My stern older brother… Well, there was no one like him I can tell you. I suddenly realized that I might be seeing him for the very last time, and I believe he held the same realization about me. It was not something either of us wanted to dwell upon but the feeling of approaching doom was clearly in the air. Mycroft shook it off well, as did I.

"Well then, now I'm afraid, duty calls and I must be off," Mycroft said in a loud bluster as he raised his massive bulk out of our long-suffering divan. "I have much work to do at Whitehall. The Empire never sleeps, and all that rot. Ah…good luck to you, Sherlock, and also to you, Doctor Watson. Stay alert. I shall be in touch."

Once Mycroft had gone, Watson and I were left alone in our sitting room at 221B, ensconced in silence and dire contemplative thought. There was much to think about. I was puffing away madly upon my Meerschaum, and soon the room was covered in a veritable haze of smoke. I hardly noticed. Neither did my companion, who so often chided me about my pipe smoke. This time he was completely mum about it.

My thoughts were awhirl about the horrible death of poor Kitty Winter, Johnson imprisoned on a false charge of her murder, and the very real possibility that Baron Gruner was apparently targeting me now. Where was the man? How could I find him? How could I stop him?

"So what do we do now?" Watson asked me.

"We have to find the Baron before he finds us," I said simply.

"How do we do that?"

"We make inquiries."

He nodded, looking out our front window. "Holmes, I notice a man, perhaps he is one of Mycroft's own, stationed below at the front door to 221?"

I nodded, noncommittally.

Through the other window Watson located other men on duty at both ends of Baker Street. They were certainly Mycroft's men, and the good doctor remarked upon this to me, hoping the knowledge would make *me* feel more secure. I had not the heart to dissuade him upon this news so I said nothing.

"Well, Holmes, it certainly buoys my spirits to see Mycroft's men on guard to protect us," he offered hopefully.

Finally I could hold back no longer and allowed my laugher full reign, unable to resist scoffing at those guards and what I considered to be mere *faux* protection. "I'm afraid, Watson, that when Gruner decides to make his move, nothing will be able to stop him. Not Mycroft's men, not Lestrade's', and perhaps not even us."

"That is certainly a dark tone, Holmes. So what do we do?"

"As I have said, we must find the Baron before he can act against us."

"How do we do that? Where do we look?"

"Indeed, therein lies the rub. The man is a master of subterfuge and possesses extreme cunning and vast resources. He has obviously gone to ground and is well hidden, directing his agents even as we speak."

"So then, this is some master plan he has worked on for many weeks?" Watson asked me now beginning to fully understand the enormity of our problem.

"Not weeks, nor months, I'm afraid old man, more like years...ever since the original case ended," I corrected.

"I see," Watson muttered grimly.

"I am sure he has a plan, a master plan if I dare say it, but perhaps that very plan could be made to become the downfall of Gruner."

"How so?" Watson stammered, I could see he was grasping at any hope now however thin.

"Well, that remains to be seen, but first the man must be found," I answered rather enigmatically. "I shall contact all of the usual, and many of the unusual agents available to us in an effort to discover the whereabouts of the Baron. Every one of them, from my Baker Street Irregulars, to those underworld connections I possess, to our contacts in the nobility and beyond... You can be sure that I will call in all favors owed. There are many. You may remember a special favor *is* owed us from a royal personage regarding the de Merville case?"

"You mean from her father, the General?"

"Yes, but even higher up than that," I noted simply. "Also, Mycroft's contacts at Whitehall and the Foreign Office are not inconsiderable. Someone, somewhere will get a scent of the Baron, somebody will smell him out like a trusty bloodhound. You can not hide that arrogant, debaucherous, deformed Austrian beast here in England for long without some hint of his whereabouts. At some point, someone will see something and we shall get wind of it."

"Well that is a relief, at least."

I smiled, "The only problem of course, is that he may act first. But buck up, Watson, when we hear word, we shall have him."

Watson nodded sternly. I could see that he had called upon the very spirit of his old military training so that now fierce determination shone from his face. I smiled at him and he smiled back at me.

"That's the spirit, old man! Stand firm! We shall find him. We shall get him yet, and then he shall pay for all his crimes."

"Yes, we shall best him, Holmes!" Watson barked in bold defiance. Then after a moment he looked at me curiously, and in a more subdued tone asked, "Ah...Holmes? What do we do with him once we find him? I mean, he's hardly likely to own up to all his crimes, nor admit his part in the murder of Kitty Winter and that unfortunate young rakehell, Simon Germaine, nor clear Shinwell Johnson of their murders."

"No, he is not."

"Then what?"

"He's playing with us, my friend," I explained tersely. "The vitriol was specifically used for no other purpose but to get my attention. Now he has it. Superficially its use in Kitty's murder appears to be just one more manifestation of his beastly revenge, but in fact he is sending me a clear message. He wants me to know that he did it."

"So we are in the..." Watson blurted, surprising me by his use of a rather foul expletive that amply matched my even fouler mood.

"Crudely put, old man, but there you have it, in a nutshell."

I stood up from my chair. Gave Watson a wan look and then, without any word I walked into my bedroom, softly closing the door behind me. I needed to be alone, I needed time to think. I needed to set the wheels in motion...

For the moment I sat alone in my room and silently pondered our predicament. I knew that Watson being left to his own devices would, no doubt, do some reading, or perhaps try to work on one of his stories of my cases that he was writing up for the *Strand*. However, I knew my friend only too well, I was sure that he would not be able to keep his thoughts fixed on what he was doing. His attention could not help but stray to the danger I was in from the Baron. He was consumed, no doubt as I was, by trying to determine just what mode of attack the Baron would take against me. I was sure it would give him a sleepless night, but at least he would remain here, safe at Baker Street.

For my own part I decided to forgo sleep. I knew what I had to do. So I quietly took my leave through the back window of my room in an effort not to disturb my friend and to clandestinely investigate certain possibilities about the whereabouts of Baron Gruner. I thought it best at that point to leave good old Watson behind at Baker Street and well out of danger. For I had people to see and places to be and none of them were very pleasant, nor safe.

As it turned out, it was a decision that I would rue for the rest of my days.

Chapter 6
Limehouse

*N*ormally I would do such clandestine work in one of my various disguises. I had many that were quite useful and effective to hide my identity and I employed them often for just such exigencies. But not now. There was no time for any of that now.

The door to my room was closed and I left it so. I gathered my coat and an envelope that I slipped into my inside pocket. I then silently made my way out of the back window of my bedroom. I had considered going out armed but the places where I was headed, and the people I were to be among, well, it would probably keep me safer if I did not approach them carrying a weapon. Or so I hoped. It was dangerous business without a weapon at the best of times, but sometimes it could be more dangerous having one. I'd certainly miss trusty old Watson and his revolver, but I could never allow him to be placed in such considerable jeopardy by accompanying me on the dark mission I had to perform this night.

The sad fact of the matter was that not a single one of my usual connections had turned up anything of value in my search for Baron Gruner. My Baker Street Irregulars, while all stout lads, had come up empty; Mycroft's contacts had drawn a blank; and those friendly — and even unfriendly — underworld connections I knew from long years of use had come up with nothing. It was time to try something different, more extreme, the odds indicated as much. It was time for me to delve deeper into those dark places where even I was loath to go at times, down into the grim and deadly underworld places where I had no connections at all and the very name Sherlock Holmes was met with abject hatred by those who sought only revenge for my acts against their crimes. These were the horrid dens of iniquity where I had no protection and often times a price had been placed upon my head.

Deftly I slipped through the window of my Baker Street bedroom, to alight upon the ledge where I easily dropped the few feet to the adjoining roof of the next building, then quickly down the wooden railing of the fire stairway at the floor of the alley below. In an instant I was gone, soaked up by the blackness of the foggy London night on a mission that even I could never imagine where it would lead me.

I had been doing a gadabout job of going through the various dark dens of the London underworld, going from one terrible place to the next, speaking carefully among shifty criminals and deadly fallen women, getting names, following leads. I kept at it hour after hour, following more leads and talking to the worst sort London had to offer, all of which were as suspicious of me as I was as careful not to turn my back on them. They all readily took the cash I offered for their information. Some of the worst lured me in and tried to take me down for the cash I had on me, but none of them were fast enough or able to surprise me for a moment with their game. They never even laid a finger on me, but this was still getting me nowhere and the night was passing fast.

It was exhausting work, the hours slipping by and I feared I was wasting valuable time. I had a few hours left this night before I must get back to Baker Street and Watson. I had to make a contact, find a lead, somehow, somewhere. The trail so far had been dead, and that fact alone told me one thing I needed to consider. There was one place I had yet to try. My needs led me just naturally to that place, London's lowest den of criminal activity, the notorious Limehouse Pub.

The place was a disgusting den of sloth and sin run by a wily criminal named Shank Frobish. The man was dangerous in the extreme, one of the last minions of the old Moriarty gang who was still loose in London and still plying his various illegal trades with seemingly impervious security. 'Old Shank' as he was called, had only once been placed in prison, and that time only because of evidence I had discovered and turned over to the police to put him securely in a cell he so justly deserved. He served his time and was let out. Of course, he still hated me and openly boasted that he would kill me one day. It is said he had even placed a price upon my head. I smiled. He was not the first to do so and he would not be the last.

I knew wily Shank Frobish well; he would never help me voluntarily. In fact, he might just shoot me dead on sight — he hated me with a passion he could barely restrain since my taking down of his master, Moriarty some years back. That, with his time in prison, did not endear me to him —

Deftly I slipped through the window of my Baker Street bedroom.

all of which had also deeply cut into his wealth, at the same time growing his anger against me considerably. Nevertheless, there was still one thing I was counting on with wily Old Shank. Shank was a practical criminal; he never put personal animosity over the lure of obtaining filthy lucre. Shank was a cash-on-the-barrelhead fellow and no questions asked, Devil take the hindmost, so I decided to try him for the answers I needed, in spite of the obvious danger.

I knew I'd be entering the vilest den of thieves and cutthroats in all of London without any disguise as to my true identity — a place where anyone there — or all of them — might take my life if they could. Of course, I had taken precautions, but sometimes the best precautions are for naught. I had no choice now. I was at my wits end in my search for Baron Gruner and my list of leads was almost gone. I needed to find a new field to reap.

The domain was dark and smoky, loud and full of drunken wild song. As I said, I was not wearing any of my usual disguises this time around, so no sooner did I enter the doorway of the sordid establishment than all talk and laughter suddenly stopped. The looks that flashed between the customers and upon their faces told me that they all knew me. Sherlock Holmes had dared enter their private pub and the glares of utter hatred were palpable. I recognized no less than a dozen of the most loathsome denizens of the London underworld seated at tables right before me, whom I had put into prison at one time or another through my various cases. I slowly walked into the insidious den of criminal evil with my head held high and with a level of confidence I did not truly feel, even as I noticed weapons being slowly drawn; revolvers suddenly slipping out of hidden pockets in thick coats; shiny knives grasped in twitching eager hands. I readied myself, set to go into a defensive *baritsu* fight stance and battle for my life if need be when I heard a powerful voice boom out like a lord from very Olympus itself.

"Wot 'ave we 'ere!" The voice suddenly blared loudly from behind the bar. "Not the famous Sherlock 'Olmes, upon my word!'

It was Old Shank Frobish himself. The huge Irishman had noticed me as soon as I had entered his pub and had already given the signal to his people to make sure they followed his order. Or else. Whether that order would be to kill me in a melee of guns and knives I was not sure. Things certainly looked grim. Perhaps coming here had been a mistake, but I decided to brave it through, much like good old Watson would do, and play the tough British bulldog to the hilt.

The large Irishman's voice and manner instantly drew the attention of all men and women there to his attention. He smiled at me. It was a grim look of utter doom.

I nodded, it was his play now.

"Leave 'im to me!" Frobish's voice boomed out in powerful wrath to everyone in the place. It was an unmistakable order none could resist. "I say, leave 'im be, or you'll be tasting my wrath!"

There were groans and moans of displeasure, the men at the tables scowled in anger and bitter disappointment but the drawn and aimed revolvers were suddenly uncocked and carefully placed back into hidden coat pockets; the knives were slowly sheathed to disappear as if they had never been pulled out in the first place. Eyes reluctantly turned away from me and most of the men returned to their drink, their women, and their conversations.

I walked over to Shank Frobish. He stood behind the bar waiting for me. He was not holding a weapon, but I was certain that he had one on him that he could withdraw in the blink of an eye should he need it. Shank was nothing, if not prepared.

"You! You of all people dare to enter my pub!" Frobish growled at me. "And you do not even give me the respect of sneaking inside as you have in the past in your usual disguises. You have a lotta nerve, Mr. Sherlock 'Olmes!"

I walked closer, bellied up to the bar and looked closely at Frobish speaking sharply, "That could have been nasty with your people back there. Glad you called them off. Or did you do so, only to save me for yourself?"

"Aye, nasty for you, not for me, Mr. 'Olmes. But as for you and me, I'll bide me time for the moment. Surely you 'ave the smell of death upon you, but I smell something stronger and even more to my liking than your death, and that be cash. Am I right?"

I nodded.

"Then I assume you're 'ere for information? I know you well. Do you 'ave the dosh on you?"

"I can pay well for what I require."

Frobish smiled now, "Ever me way, Mr. 'Olmes, give me the quid and I'll give you the talk o' the town if ye like."

"I don't require the talk of the town. I just need to know the whereabouts of one man."

Frobish nodded, it seemed simple enough. He waited. He could be patient when the need arose.

"Baron Adelbert Gruner," I stated plainly.

I saw the cocky look on Old Shank's face change appreciably and disappear. It was not exactly fear I saw there, for Shank Frobish feared no man, but there was serious concern there in his eyes. It was the respect of one jungle predator for another one who could be just as deadly. He looked at me carefully. "You don't ask for much, do you? That's a 'ard one, Mr. 'Olmes."

"I know, that is why I am willing to pay such a high price."

Frobish thought this over for a minute, then nodded, he liked what he was hearing but he still kept mum.

"I know he is in England, maybe even here in London," I insisted, trying to egg him on.

"Well, I ain't sayin' 'e is, and I ain't sayin' 'e ain't," Frobish leered, his black rotted teeth making his mouth appear as foul as he and his dubious establishment surely were. He took out two glasses and poured two drinks, pushing one over to me, then he quickly downed his own.

"Drink with me," he said.

I did not touch my drink. I did not need to be poisoned or slipped a drug just then. I had seen the man's quick movement; that he had dropped something into my glass. The man was good at his game.

"I didn't come here to drink with you, Shank. I asked you a question and I want an answer," I went for my inside coat pocket and saw the man immediately flinch, then suddenly pull out a revolver that he pointed squarely at my face. We stood face to face frozen like that for a long moment. The pub suddenly got very quiet again and all eyes were now upon us.

"Kill the blighter, Shank!" one of the denizens shouted.

"Plug the rotter dead!" another man demanded.

I stood my ground nervous but solid, waiting for Shank to make his move. I didn't want him to kill me of course, and I didn't want to kill him either, what I wanted was information. And I was ready to pay for it. However, I realized my movement towards my coat pocket for the cash had been made too rapidly and spooked him.

"I could shoot you dead right 'ere, Mr. 'Olmes. I'd enjoy doing it too."

"Yes, but then you would lose out on a lot of money, Mr. Frobish."

"Money? How much?"

I smiled, slowly withdrew a wad of ten pound notes. "I am unarmed. This is what I had reached into my pocket for. Five hundred pounds."

Shank looked at the cash carefully, nodded, put his revolver away ready to talk business now. He could always shoot me later, I was sure he was thinking.

Shank next barked out a loud demand to his customers, "You all mind your own damn business!"

The order was unmistakable in its menace. The denizens of the Limehouse Pub all looked away from us to resume their talking and drinking. A moment later no one was paying any attention to us at all where we stood alone, he behind the bar and I in front.

"That's a lot of dosh," he said tensely, his eyes still focused upon the wad of bills lustfully. I held the bills in my hand just out of his reach. His lips smacked nervously and his tongue darted in and out of his mouth while his eyes never left the bills I held in front of him.

"I need information," I reminded him. "I'm willing to pay for what I need."

"Oh, you'll pay, you will! But you're not asking for much. The Baron's a difficult fellow, 'e's got agents all over town, and 'e's gone to ground I 'ear," Old Shank grinned, showing me his blackened teeth and trying to feign an aura of cooperation. I knew that was when such a man was at his most dangerous. "Place the money on the bar, Mr. 'Olmes."

"You want to tell me where the Baron is, Mr. Frobish?"

He laughed then, "'ell, I could just drop you now with one well-placed shot and take the damn dosh. It's my place, no one would dare say a word against me and it would do me soul good to put an end to the great Sherlock 'Olmes."

I smiled, "No doubt it would, but then you would lose out on all the money due to you when I catch the Baron. It would be considerable."

"Considerable, you say? Like what does that mean? More than the five 'undred quid?"

"Oh, considerably more, Shank," I told him with a grim smile. I knew my man, and while I knew of his severe hatred for me, I knew that could sometimes be eclipsed by his severe desire for cash — especially lots of it. I could see his mind scheming now, weighing the short term pleasure of my murder and taking my five hundred quid, against a larger sum of cash to be gained later. Like I say, Old Shank was wily, a practical criminal.

"So 'ow much you taking about?"

"Ten times what I will give you now."

"Blimey! That's five thousand quid!"

"So you game?"

Shank sighed, "Drop the wad on the bar and promise me to be paid that considerable amount when you catch your man. I know you're a man of your word, so I'll take you at your word. What do you say?"

"Done," I said, dropping the bills on the bar top.

Shank Frobish smiled, picked up my five hundred pounds and stashed the bills into his shirt. Then he leaned in closer to me, and in a low whisper said, "I don't know much. I 'ear tell though that 'e 'as a man what works for 'im, another foreigner, a big tall man, name of Sergey."

"Yes, go on," I insisted, excited now, knowing I was on the right track and that I had my first real lead to the Baron. Porky had mentioned a man named Sergey, who he said was also a foreigner. If I could find this Sergey, then he might lead me to the Baron. Or such was my hope.

"Tell me about this Sergey?" I demanded.

Old Shank whispered harshly, drawing in closer, "Not much to tell. 'e comes 'ere sometimes. For the ladies, you know? When 'e drinks, 'e talks, and last time 'e talked, then laughed about what 'appened to Kitty and Porky. Well, I didn't like that kind of talk much, seeing as Kitty and Porky are known around 'ere and liked. They was Limehouse people just like all of us 'ere but this Sergey just talked on 'ow 'e did them dirty. A nasty piece of work 'e is. Laughed at 'ow the girl was killed."

"He did?"

"Aye."

"So you don't like him?"

"Well, I don't like many people, Mr. 'Olmes, you know that. I don't like you at all, but you 'ave cash for me, so I am making some allowances... Any'ow, I don't like foreigners to begin with either, and then I don't like them that brings trouble to me own people 'ere in Limehouse. I 'ave no loyalty for the likes of someone like that."

I nodded, "Where can I find him?"

"They say this Sergey has a crib two blocks down from 'ere. The man takes 'im a doxy there from time to time for fun and games. You knows what I mean? The number is 349, down the street, Mr. 'Olmes."

I nodded, "All right then, if this leads me to the Baron you'll have you're considerable reward."

"Don't forget me. Mr. 'Olmes. I know where you live. Remember, you're leaving 'ere alive under my personal protection, still a living, breathing soul — when there's many men 'ere — including my ownself — who'd just as soon put you in a grave."

"If your information is true then you shall be amply rewarded, Mr. Frobish."

Shank Frobish nodded, "Then go in peace, Mr. 'Olmes."

I was startled when I heard the man's deep bass voice boom out to his customers with what could only be termed imperial orders, "I warns you all 'ere and now, anyone touches that man, it be upon pain o' death! Listen to wot I say! Leave 'im be, for now!"

I saw the customers were mightily upset by Old Shank's order but they obeyed it, even as they clearly growled with disappointment. They did as they were told and looked away from me, none anxious to cross wily Old Shank Frobish, especially not in his own pub. That would be a measure of disrespect that would get them a death sentence. So I felt a bit safer that I could spot not one man draw a revolver, and there were no knives in view, which caused me to silently sigh with relief. I walked out of the Limehouse Pub into the dark fog of the London night.

Making sure no one followed me, I headed the three blocks to number 349. The building was another shambles, small, dirty and dingy, the window glass broken and boarded up. I realized such a place would make a perfect trap. Perhaps even now Sergey and the Baron's men — maybe even Gruner himself — were waiting inside to murder me? But while it might be a trap, I considered Shank Frobish's words about not liking foreigners, and not liking what he had heard done to Kitty and Porky. They were Limehouse people, just like he was. There was a bond of some type there I was sure. And while Frobish might like nothing better than to kill Sherlock Holmes — there was that one thing he liked even better — and that was money. I just hoped my promise of five thousand pounds was enough to assuage his feelings of being cheated of my murder. I also hoped that the wily fellow had not made some deal with the Baron to lead me into a trap here. While always possible, I thought that was not likely. Frobish had my money on his mind. So I felt I was relatively safe from him, at least for the present. I could not pay him if he turned me over to the Baron.

Now, as to the Baron and this lead on Sergey...

I sighed thoughtfully, looking closely at number 349. It was so dark and quiet, and for a moment I reconsidered that perhaps I should have carried my revolver with me on this trip. And while I secretly longed for Watson's stout comradeship and his own trusty revolver, I was still vastly relieved that he was not here with me now but safely back at home at Baker Street. If things here turned deadly, at least he was safe.

It was time. I looked around me at the foggy Limehouse streets. It was pitch dark and dank with fog all over, with few people around. The perfect time and place for a murder — perhaps the murder of Sherlock Holmes?

I had almost been killed twice tonight; once by the angry mob at the Limehouse Pub and once by Shank Frobish, so perhaps as the old saying goes, 'three's a charm?' I smiled with grim irony but firm determination. So be it. Nothing was going to stop me from tracking down Baron Gruner and if entering this room — this possible trap — would bring me closer to him then I would go willingly where it led me. I knew I had to enter number 349 and see what I would discover there.

I carefully approached the door, reached out to grasp the handle. I slowly turned it. It was unlocked. Alarm bells rang in my mind once again warning me that this could be a trap, but I knew I had no recourse now but to enter that room and see what was there for myself. I did.

I opened the door. It made a resounding groan, as disconcerting as a coffin lid being opened. The room was dark. Quiet. I was actually surprised that no one hit me over the head, no one shot me, no one even spoke — though I had expected such and was ready to fight back if need be. Instead there was no one in that room but I. There was no mysterious Sergey. There was no Baron Gruner. There was no one but myself. I sighed, whether from disappointment or relief I could not tell at that point. I carefully walked into the room and then slowly closed the door behind me. I lit a match.

Walking a few steps I found some candles and began lighting them to illuminate the small squalid room. It wasn't much, a broken bed and old mattress, a small dirty table, and a small dresser with three drawers up against the far wall.

Once my eyes became accustomed to the candlelight I noticed the place was nothing but a dingy flop and that it was not only uninhabited, but that it had been so for some time. Whoever had been living here had since moved out and taken all their things. It appeared the man had left nothing behind, but I knew appearances could often be deceiving. Still and all, I discovered no clothing, no papers, not much of anything that would help me in my quest. I began an intense search of the premises. There was some time left, so after my superficial overview of the place, making sure I missed nothing, I began a more detailed investigation. I took out my magnifying glass to examine the floor under the bed, to check the mattress of the bug-ridden bed. I even cut open the mattress with my penknife for anything hidden within. There was nothing. Next I carefully examined the wooden table, especially the wood of the tabletop which had multiple knife marks gouged into it; there were various initials, words, designs. All of which did not mean anything to me at the moment, though

I filed them away for possible future use. I moved over to examine the small dresser set against the far wall. I pulled out all three of the empty wooden drawers and closely ran my eyes over them. I took particular note to discover if anything had been affixed to the bottom of these drawers. There was nothing.

I moved the dresser away from its spot against the wall — and there I found it! Behind the dresser. On the face of things it was not much at all, apparently meaningless, but I knew better. It was a simple calling card, but not just any calling card; this was a quality item on embossed paper printed in gold flake ink. It was a calling card for Her Excellency, The Countess Alexa Von Huenfeld. I had read about her in *The Times*. The dowager Countess they called her, an elderly grand dame of old German nobility, she had lately taken up residence in the Kentish countryside for her health. In fact, she had taken a rather elegant house, quite large to be sure. I even remember noting the fact to good Watson at the time when I read the announcement in the press, mentioning to my friend that it seemed rather a bit much for only herself and the small retinue that accompanied her to England. I put the card into my pocket.

If Sergey had indeed used this crib while in London, and if he did work for the Baron as I assumed, then the Baron might be somehow associated with the Countess.

I knew of the house, which had been a former palace of the Stuarts, and it seemed to me just the isolated type of place that Gruner might find useful for his needs — a secure bolt hole for him to hide in while he pursued his sordid plans of revenge against me. So it seemed to me that I had come upon a promising lead and that it needed to be looked into. However, the joy of this discovery was blunted somewhat by the fact that the home the Countess had taken was far off in Kent. Getting to it would entail some time and distance in travel from London. I could not look into it this night. In fact, my time this night was severely limited and it was fast approaching dawn. I wanted to get back to my room at Baker Street before the morning. As it was, I would no doubt be late but I was gratified that I had at least discovered one promising lead to share with Watson.

Chapter 7
The Murder of Doctor Watson

he more I thought about what I had just learned, the more I was determined to return to Baker Street by early morning, collect faithful Watson, and at once have us take a train down to Kent to investigate this German countess. Then if I found Gruner I would alert Lestrade, see to it Johnson was set free, and then close the case once and for all.

Alas, it was not to be.

It was with this plan in mind that I carefully crawled through the back window of my bedroom at 221, easily bypassing Mycroft's guardian posted at the front door and those at both ends of Baker Street. No need to bother with them with my movements, they had not even noted my exit, nor my return.

It was late night, soon to be dawn but as expected my room was pitch black as I entered. The door closed, just as I had left it. Nothing unusual. Except... I was curious to notice a small wet spot upon the window sill. I casually wondered about this as I carefully closed the window behind me and entered my room. Once inside the room, I was determined to get a lamp and make a closer examination of the strange wet spot that I knew surely had to be a drop of blood. It was a curious discovery and instantly piqued my alarm of course, but by then it was too late.

Suddenly the lights went on and I was shocked to see Inspector Lestrade framed in the now open doorway to my room, a group of stout London Bobbies behind him.

"Lestrade?"

"I'm afraid I am here to arrest you, Mr. Holmes," The Scotland Yard inspector told me plainly, and damn his eyes if he was not deadly serious.

"Arrest me? For what?"

He looked at me with a hard, cold gaze I had never seen from him before.

I am sure you can imagine my surprise, for his words fairly took my breath away, but it is what he said next that sent me reeling in shock as if struck with a sledgehammer.

"I am here to arrest you for the murder of Doctor John H. Watson."

"Surely you jest!" I asked, completely astounded.

Lestrade's dour look told me differently, "I've never been more serious in my life."

I was speechless.

Watson?

Dead?

Murdered?

"This is impossible!" I blurted allowing my anger to show now, but then I thought of the Baron and suddenly grew worried. Was it, in fact, possible?

"Constables, please escort Mr. Holmes downstairs to the beetle." Lestrade ordered his men. Then to me he added softly, "Please, Mr. Holmes, don't make it any harder on me and my men by resisting. I am loath to order them to use cuffs and shackles unless it is necessary."

"Watson!" I shouted, then I muttered softly, "John is dead?"

"Aye."

"How did this happen?" I cried.

"How, indeed, Mr. Holmes," Lestrade answered enigmatically.

I looked at him in shock, curious, "What do you mean by that?"

"He is dead. I am sorry. You may view the body on the way out if you like, but you are not to approach it, nor touch it in any way," Lestrade stated with a combination of sadness and anger I had never seen in him before which he seemed to hold in check with great difficulty.

What had happened here in my absence?

I looked at the inspector aghast, my mind reeling.

What could it all mean?

What had happened here while I had been away?

Then it came to me. I should have realized it at once.

Oh, why did I not see this coming?

It was really quite simple. By killing Kitty the Baron had finished Porky

"I am here to arrest you for the murder of Doctor John H. Watson."

off, and by killing Watson he had finished me off. He had set up Porky and myself for his own form of revenge killings. It was brilliant. It was bestial. I was stunned by the news of Watson's murder, horrified at his death, deadened in my very heart.

Lestrade told me, "I know how close you two have been over the years, good friends and all, but everyone has their falling outs at times. I can understand that, I guess. Arguments happen and can get out of hand with disastrous results that no one intended, nor ever anticipated."

"No," I mumbled. "This is not possible."

Lestrade continued coldly, "Mrs. Hudson heard the entire fight quite clearly, your voice raised in anger, Watson's pleas for mercy. She called me straight away. We have your letter opener, the murder weapon. I am sure analysis will show it is your fingerprints upon it, and Watson's blood. It was found lying upon your bed. You must have dropped it there as you fled. There was more blood on the doorknob to your bedroom and also upon the window sill of your room. I am sorry, Mr. Holmes, but this changes everything."

I stood there stunned as they walked me out into our sitting room. I was totally shocked and reeling from the news, and then my eyes fell upon a body lying lifeless upon the floor. The power of a dozen opium pipes could not have created the lethargy and sadness that hit me then.

"Watson!" I cried. "John!"

I saw Watson's lifeless body lying upon our sitting room floor, there could be no doubt about it. He lay there right in front of his favorite chair, the chair directly across from my own. He was dressed in the same clothes he had been wearing when I had left our rooms so many hours before. I even noticed his father's beloved old pocket watch in the open palm of his hand, as if he had been keeping track for the time of my return.

"Watson!" I screamed unable to hold back my rage and pain. How had this happened! I stared at the body from where I stood held back between two stout Bobbies. It appeared to be Watson without any doubt, but there was something wrong with his face, it seemed to be terribly disfigured for some reason. As I viewed the mutilated body, I reflected that the only blessing was that Watson's late wife Mary was not alive to see her husband's terrible end.

By then I knew of course.

At once it all became clear to me.

Vitriol had been used.

The mark of Baron Gruner!

That sealed my fate.

"John!" I shouted nearly apoplectic with shock. At that moment I am afraid to say that I lost my celebrated tact and logic, lost all that for which I have strived my entire life and career to master as a consulting detective. I shouted wildly, enraged by what the Baron had done and tried vainly to get close to the body of my friend, but a stout brace of Bobbies held me firmly in check.

"Stop! Stop, Mr. Holmes! I implore you!" I heard a voice order.

"I must examine the body!" I demanded.

"No! You shall not! You must contain yourself, Mr. Holmes," Lestrade said sternly, patient but firm. "You will not be allowed to approach the doctor's body. That body is evidence now, which you are denied to meddle with. If you can not calm yourself, I shall have to resort to the manacles."

Lestrade's words were like a cold slap to my face. I took a deep breath, replacing my rage and sense of tragic loss with the realization that I needed more than ever now to rely upon my deductive facilities for good old Watson's sake. To avenge his murder. Gruner would pay for this!

I stood motionless looking down at my old friend as the Bobbies held me and Lestrade looked upon the murder scene. Both of us stood there in disbelief and were silent for a long moment.

Finally Lestrade explained, "You can see he has been stabbed no less than six times. It was done in anger, a fight or disagreement between the two of you. Can you tell me what it was about?"

I said nothing, I was still in shock, there was nothing for me to say. I could not even voice the words of denial or explain that this had all been done by Baron Gruner. Not yet. The truth was, Watson was dead now, and nothing I might tell Lestrade about the Baron and his plan could bring my friend back. Nothing else seemed to matter at that point.

Lestrade continued, "As I've said, your letter opener was the murder weapon. I'm sorry, Mr. Holmes, I'm sorry that it has come to this."

"Vitriol?" I asked softly.

"Eh?" Lestrade said. "What was that you said?"

"His face has been eaten away by Vitriol?"

"Vitriol, or some such sulfate acid," Lestrade agreed and I could see the disgust grow upon his face. "I examined the small chemistry laboratory you have set up at the corner table yonder. Quite impressive. It appears that the acid used to disfigure Doctor Watson's face originated there. We have found a beaker, Mr. Holmes, with some of the acid remaining within it. I'm afraid it further links you to the murder."

"Of course. Yes, it all makes perfect sense."

"Well, I'd not be so glib about it all, Mr. Holmes. I mean, using acid on the doctor like that, it was really uncalled for, not the gentlemanly thing to do at all, regardless of your rage or reason," Lestrade stated, holding his own anger in check with obvious difficulty.

I looked at the Inspector sharply, "Are you serious, Lestrade? Do you actually believe I did this? Do you really believe that I could kill Doctor Watson? If so, you are an idiot!"

"Mr. Holmes, no need for insults. We have the evidence and the evidence does not lie. You have told me so many times."

"No, but you know that evidence can be *made* to lie," I replied sharply.

"Not so in this case, I'm afraid, Mr. Holmes. This is not the entirety of the evidence we possess against you. There is more, much more. It appears this case shall be open and shut rather quickly, I foresee," he said with a confidence that for once I admit shook my own, for I realized the Baron had done his work well and had set me up perfectly.

"The Baron did this, Lestrade," I told him softly, looking into his eyes, pleading.

"The Baron, you say? This Baron is reported to be home in Austria, Mr. Holmes. There is absolutely nothing to indicate that he is in London at all. He is not even in England. No, I'm afraid the evidence speaks for itself."

I sighed deeply, deflated and apparently defeated. I had made an effort at an explanation to Lestrade but he would not listen, and in all truth at that point poor John's death weighed so heavily upon my thoughts that I did not care all that much just then what happened to me. I realized now that the Baron had taken out his revenge against me in the only way that would ever truly hurt me — not with *my* murder as I had so foolishly assumed — but with the murder of my best friend, the best friend any man ever had in this world or any other — Doctor John H. Watson.

I took one last look at poor Watson where his body lay so brutalized in death upon the floor of our flat and said my goodbye silently, mouthing a little prayer. The sadness I felt was indescribable, it was a terrible weight that pressed upon my chest, upon my heart, upon my very soul. I suddenly felt dizzy. The world seemed to swirl around me. I felt the Bobbies grasp me in an effort to help hold me upright.

"Easy there, Guv'nor," one of the constables said to me. I grew unaccountably dizzy, light-headed, while a fear and panic seized me that I had never felt before.

"Best get him out of here now," I heard Lestrade order his men gruffly.

"Damn tragedy it is to have something like this happen, not to mention the end of a brilliant career."

I remember the Bobbies leading me out of our rooms and down the stairs. Below I saw Mrs. Hudson. Good old, Mrs. Hudson. Surely she knew that I could never do such a thing.

She was crying wildly, then screamed once she saw me being lead down the stairs towards her. She was almost hysterical and I felt mightily for her. I assume she had been the one to first come upon Watson's body, so it must have been a terrible shock for her.

Mrs. Hudson looked up at me curiously as I was lead down the stairs and passed her. I looked into her tearful eyes, our eyes met, sadness meeting sadness.

"Why, Mr. Holmes?" she cried, clutching my arm. "How could you?"

I stammered slowly, "I did not do it."

"Oh, Mr. Holmes… he's gone…" she cried, shaken to her very core. Then she suddenly rallied in anger, "Why did you two have to fight? I heard his voice myself, plain as day. He asked you to put down the knife. He pleaded with you. His last words were, 'Please, no, Sherlock! You will kill me!' Then he died. You killed him!"

I was shocked by Mrs. Hudson's words. Even my own loyal housekeeper of so many years now believed I had murdered Watson. It was so very disheartening.

Then the constables took me out of 221 for perhaps the last time, placing me in the back of a police van that took me away to Scotland Yard. I remember little of the ride. My mind was a whirlwind of dark confusion and bleak heartbreak.

Once I arrived at Scotland Yard — this time not as the world-renowned consulting detective, the valued peer in criminal investigation as in the past — but as just a another vile criminal, and a murderous one at that — I found myself in quite a different situation. The realization caused my heart to sink even deeper into despair. They quickly processed me for arrest, then placed me alone in a jail cell, down in a deep corner of the building. I was thankful, at least, that I was placed away from all the other prisoners. Alone.

I could tell Lestrade was just as shocked as I by the murder of Watson. He was taken by genuine sadness by the crime, and the sheer brutality of it, but I saw no pity in his eyes for me, only anger. It was an anger I had never seen in the man before.

This then, no doubt, was now the end of the Great Detective, Sherlock Holmes.

"I will alert your brother as to what has happened," Lestrade told me curtly, then he closed the door to my jail cell and silently walked away. I listened as his footsteps as they echoed down that long, lonely hall until they had diminished into nothing — as I feared was also the case with me now.

Now I was alone with my thoughts, haunted by so very many demons.

I hardly remember much of what happened that first day. It all appeared as a monstrous blur, obfuscated by so many powerful emotions and tragic regrets that it was impossible for me to fully get a grip on them all and sort them out. Chief among these was the thought that what had occurred had all been my fault. For I had left Watson behind, alone at Baker Street.

Now that I thought it through, it seemed so wrong, such a tragic mistake. However, at the time — where I was going and with what I had to do — I did not want him to be placed in danger. Ironic, is it not? I let out a grim groan at the terrible irony of it all — that at the time, I had thought it would be too dangerous for my friend to accompany me to seek the Baron's whereabouts.

I assumed he would be safe at Baker Street.

I must admit that in my wildest dreams I never thought Baron Gruner would come for *Watson* — I thought only that he must come for *me*. But in the end he did come for me — *through* Watson.

I held back my sadness and tried to think things through logically, but it was more difficult than I ever imagined. I had been cut to the quick and my emotions ran rampant. Watson's murder had left me weak and languid, caring for nothing, not even justice, not even revenge. I only wished for my pipe, even dreaming of the cocaine needle. Surely a seven percent solution would make things better? Then I remembered Watson's stern admonishment against my use of the drug and steeled my nerves. He was dead and gone and I cursed myself now for my cold heart and selfish weakness.

I had to admit it; everything had been done most masterfully. It was done without mistake, perfectly in the manner of Baron Gruner to arrange events in this particular way. The vitriol was his calling card, used once again to mock me. It had become his *modus operandi*. The fact that my own small chemistry lab now seemed to validate my use of the acid upon poor Watson was just one more stroke against me. And yet, Gruner had perpetuated this crime of crimes and set it all up in such a way that Lestrade — even ever- faithful Mrs. Hudson! — quite readily believed that I had murdered my best friend. It was diabolical.

Of course I soon learned that the popular press became utterly rabid with the sensational story in spite of Mycroft's considerable influence to kill the scandal. But a scandal it surely was, a scandal unlike anything of the time.

The next day Mycroft brought me newspapers with headlines that blazed in red ink:

FAMOUS PRIVATE DETECTIVE MURDERS BEST FRIEND!

And above the fold on another:

WILL SHERLOCK HOLMES GET THE ROPE?

It was dire.

I read the various newspapers, all crammed full of articles telling the grisly details of Watson's murder almost as if the writers had been there themselves. Such utter balderdash! Many writers seemed to delight in the tragedy a bit too much, or delved far too deeply into the goriest details. One article in particular, had the effrontery to say the following:

Mr. Sherlock Holmes of London, the famous Consulting Detective, even went so far as to disfigure the face of his poor victim and long-time friend with sulfuric acid — so great was his monstrous rage and wrath! This proves to all that his jealously and hatred of the poor defenseless doctor must have been monumental indeed!

That one had me breathing fire for hours.

I read all these reports and more, with despair and utter amazement. Truth and accuracy in reporting did not seem to matter to these writers. Most of the articles were off the mark entirely and reeked of the worst aspects of purple prose and yellow journalism. Others were just bizarre fantasy and made-up supposition created out of wholecloth; the type of thing that a low-rent Jules Verne or some drug-addled Edgar Allen Poe *poseur* might put to paper.

Of course Mycroft saw to it that I was able to obtain the best legal help that money could buy. My brother spared no expense and never wavered in his support for me, but I hardly noticed any of this those first few days. My best friend in the world, and the best man I had ever known, was dead. Gone from me forever. Nothing else seemed to matter.

The sting in the ointment of course was that everyone thought that I had done the terrible deed, and because of that, I would likely find myself having an appointment with the hangman's noose some day in the future. I did not dwell upon that now of course, for I just sank deeper into despair, and perhaps self pity.

Perhaps if I was *lucky* — the word hardly seemed to have any meaning for me now — and Mycroft's influence counted for something, I might avoid a death sentence and end my life by rotting away in some prison. Perhaps exile in a penal colony in far off Australia? Either way, the prospects were grim. But as I have told you I did not care. Watson was dead. There seemed no reason to live, no reason even to fight Gruner now. He'd won handily.

Watson was gone, and soon I knew, so would I.

I was rather astonished how little my predicament mattered to me as the days passed. I found that I felt no great desire to even keep on living in a world without my good friend in it. I held no obsessive desire for justice, or to obtain revenge upon the Baron for what he had done. What did it matter now? It surely would not bring back Watson. And the fact that all of England — all the world now — thought that I had killed my best friend, meant little to me in that context. What cared I for what *they* thought — or for what anyone thought? I had no pride now, no bold arrogance. John H. Watson was dead and nothing else mattered to me.

Of course, my brother, Mycroft, came to see me as soon as he heard what had happened. He returned each morning, trying to bolster my spirits, arranging my defense, desperately seeking to find some way he could change my situation. First thing, he strove to obtain my release before the trial, but the seriousness of the charge and the severity of the murder trumped any compassion that my reputation and my brother's contacts might allow me.

Of course I brought up the fact that I had not even been in our Baker Street rooms the time of the murder but had been out looking for the Baron. I mentioned Shank Frobish and the denizens of the Limehouse Pub. "They all saw me there, Mycroft. Surely Frobish will remember me?"

I stated.

Mycroft looked into this, of course, and brought me dire news the next day. "Shank Frobish was found dead last night. The pub was set ablaze by persons unknown. It is a ruin. I have had inquiries made in the district but no one remembers you being there on the night in question — or they're not talking. It seems someone has put the fear of death into them all. None are coming forward. I'm sorry, Sherlock."

"So Shank Frobish is no more. One more victim for the Baron's growing death tally," I said, despondent.

I was later informed that I was not to be allowed release on bail. That surely was the last nail in my coffin and the end of any hope I had to set things right. For without my release before trial, I was effectively stymied in my search for Baron Gruner and unable to find a way to clear myself of the murder charge against me.

Checkmate!

I could well imagine the smile on the Baron's face.

"I tell you, Sherlock," Mycroft bellowed at me on one of his many visits to my jail cell. "We'll fight this! We'll win it! Its pure poppy-cock that anyone could believe you killed Doctor Watson. Utterly preposterous!"

"The papers all seem to believe it," I replied softly. I was in a dark mood.

"The papers! The popular press! Those sanctimonious idiots!" Mycroft barked in anger. He surely had his dander up now and it did bolster my spirits to see him so keen for me, so steadfast in his complete support. I knew he hated to see me despondent but I could not rally fully. Not yet.

"The people seem to have turned against me too," I added with my usual stoicism.

"That is rubbish I tell you," my brother told me sternly. "We will find evidence."

"Find Gruner," I told him.

Mycroft sighed, "We are trying. He has gone to ground, Sherlock, in deep hiding. We are checking all leads."

"What of that German countess?"

Mycroft looked dejected, "She's legitimate. I sent one of my best men there two days ago under cover. He reported the old girl is genuinely of the nobility, not only that, but she's a member of the German royal family. Her line goes back to Bismarck. But I'll look deeper, I promise you."

"What of Lestrade?" I asked curious to discover if the official police were looking for the Baron. I'd not seen the Inspector since he had first placed me in this cell over a week before. I assumed he was busy with police business, but now I wondered if he was avoiding me. His anger at me had been great and just as surely misplaced, but it was nonetheless real to him.

Mycroft's eyes looked down, trying to cover what I plainly saw as his own despair and hopelessness at my plight. "That dolt? Lestrade will not consider anything concerning Baron Gruner. I have gone into it with him numerous times. But with no record of Gruner even being in the country he will hear nothing of it. He says the evidence against you speaks true."

"Hah!" I shouted. "So I am effectively and neatly trapped."

"We'll find a way out of this, Sherlock. I promise you."

"Thank you, Mycroft," I said with deep affection and gratitude for all my brother's valiant efforts. "We must find Gruner before it is too late, then make him talk."

"We will, Sherlock, we will," he said softly, but there was not much passion in his voice just then. He looked at me closely, "Right now, we need your cooperation. You must work with your defense. Work with your barristers, talk to them, they are here to help you. They're good men, hand picked by me."

"Oh, very well, I'll see them."

"Thank you," Mycroft said, rising with a huff from his seat upon my jail cell cot. "And now I have to be off. Working on your defense has become something of a full-time job these days."

"I am sorry."

"Sorry? No, not at all, that's what brothers are for. I just wish I could get my hands around Baron Gruner's neck and squeeze the dirty truth out of him," my older brother said it with a wink, showing me uncharacteristic passion.

"Thank you, Mycroft, you are the best brother that a man could have."

"Oh posh... Please now, Sherlock, don't go getting all emotional on me. Remember when we were children? You always managed to get yourself into some kind of trouble. We'd have a terrible row about it afterwards, but we are still brothers and we always will be," then he grabbed my shoulder firmly and held it tightly in his huge bear-like hands. "Damn it, man, don't despair! We will come through this in the end, just as we always have."

I wished I could be as certain of the outcome as my brother appeared to be. I knew he was keeping up a brave front for my benefit and trying to buoy my spirits. Then he left me alone with my deep, dark thoughts.

Time managed to pass, the hours into days, the days into weeks.

Chapter 8
The Plot Thickens

he lights were all off and the cells were dark, quiet, and empty in my section of the jail. I was doing what I did every day now in my cell, day or night — lying upon my cot, staring up at the ceiling and running the plans, mistakes, and each occurrence over and over again in my mind. It was a useless frustrating task, a whirlwind of wasted energy and effort that took me nowhere and only exhausted my senses. The reality was that I was locked away here helpless and unable to do anything about my plight, but after many hours it did lull me into blessed sleep and forgetfulness for a short time.

I was startled when I heard my name spoken in a mysterious whisper from the other end of the dark cell block. I had not been aware the police had placed any other criminals into this part of the jail, seeing as it held the "famous," now certainly infamous — and I smirked at the very thought with dark sarcasm — "Great Detective" Sherlock Holmes.

My mind focused. My attention suddenly took in my surroundings once I heard a rough rasping voice repeat more clearly, "Mr. 'Olmes? Are you there, Mr. 'Olmes?"

I was startled by that voice. It was not the guard. It came from the other end of the cell block. From another cell.

"Shinwell Johnson? Is that you?" I called back curious.

"Aye, it be me, Mr. 'Olmes. Your old friend, Porky. They moved me here last night to prepare me for my comeuppance, I imagine. You were in a dead sleep, so I had not the heart to wake you. I see that the Baron got you too."

"Yes," I admitted softly.

"I'm sorry to hear that, I truly am, and I am sorry about the doctor. I

74

heard about him too. I know you had nothing to do with his death, not like they say in all the papers. I'm sure he was murdered by the Baron, just as me Kitty was — then he set you up to take the fall. Just like me. Sorry, I am to see this, Mr. 'Olmes," he said gruffly. Then he added, "The doctor, he was a right fine bloke, for a toff."

I smiled, "Yes he was."

"Well, I hope your case goes well — at least better than mine did," Porky said in a grimmer tone. "I'm almost done for now. The trial went quick for the likes of me, the Baron set me up as a right proper patsy. With me criminal history I had no chance. They say I'm to be hung next week."

"So soon? I'm truly sorry to hear that," I said, angry at the injustice of it all. "What about an appeal?"

"No, I'm afraid not; the appeal was denied. It's all cut and dried for the likes of one like me."

"My brother Mycroft might be able to help. I could talk to him."

"No one can help me now, Mr. 'Olmes. I'm a goner!"

"Never give up hope," I told him. I didn't know what else to say. It seemed that Porky and I had a lot more in common than I'd ever thought. Both victims of the Baron both made out to be the killers of ones we loved — then both made to die for it.

"Well, at least it will be over for me soon enough, no more waiting. The waiting is the hard part," Porky told me with conciliatory good humor. "Soon enough, there will be no more worries in this world for old Porky."

"I am sorry I could not help you," I said, and there was a most powerful regret in my voice and heart. Truth be told, I felt as if I had failed him also. As I had failed poor Watson. Porky didn't deserve this fate and the fact that the Baron was going to get away with all his crimes made me so angry I could barely restrain myself.

"That's all right, sir," Johnson stammered with good grace. "I knows you done your best and God alone knows you got your own troubles now. I wish you well and hope you find a way out of them."

"I'm afraid not," I replied, hopeless realism had its hold upon me.

"I'll tell you, Mr. 'Olmes, I've done me crimes here and there, so I do not so much fear death. Maybe I'll even see me Kitty on the other side? I would like that. Heaven or hell, it matters little to one like me. What does rile me though is this, that fiend will get away with his deeds. You know him. You know what type of man he is; a bloody monster in silk clothing. Even so, how could anyone do such a thing? I understand about revenge. I'm all for revenge meself, normally, but the way he goes about it… Well, it is not a natural thing."

"You'd just pop the bloke over the head, dump him in the Thames and be done with him, eh, Porky?" I asked with a grin, for I knew the man. His directness was a form of honesty I could understand.

He laughed then, a long lusty laugh that was good to hear. I joined with him in his grim humor. It seemed to release some of the tension and fear in both of us.

"Aye, Mr. 'Olmes, a crack on the head and goodbye to all, I say. That's me way. Direct-like. That's why I never rose above me station, I didn't have the cunning of such as the Baron. Makes you wonder though, just what kind of mind such a man as he has got, doesn't it? Anyway, something to think about during those long, lonely nights here."

Then his voice grew grim with thoughts of doom and execution upon him. "Well, leastways, it won't be long now for me. Soon old Porky will be gone."

Suddenly another voice boomed out loudly.

"Hey you! Shut up! Both of you, no talking!"

It was the guard who had returned.

"Good luck, Porky. God bless you and Kitty."

"Thank you, Mr. 'Olmes, and the same to you."

"I said shut up now or you'll both feel the bite of my club!"

All talk stopped then and the cell block returned to deathly silence.

Afterwards I lay upon my cot thinking about the damnable situation that Porky found himself in. He was a career criminal and proud of it. A man who made his livelihood through crime, as other men did honest labor, but he was a decent sort in many ways. He held to his own crude code. He even had a sense of honor, which is more than Baron Gruner had with all his fine breeding and gentlemanly pretensions. Porky could also be a loyal and true bloodhound, and of course he had been nothing but a good and loyal friend to Kitty Winter. He deserved better. So did Kitty. So did Watson.

Thinking about Watson brought up so many old memories that the pain was almost indescribable. I missed my old friend more than even I realized.

Watson's funeral had been a closed family affair. It hurt that they would not allow me to pay my last respects but I could hardly blame them under the circumstances. They, each member of the family, saw me as his killer, after all.

Watson was buried at St. Johns Cemetery, beside his second wife. I am told it is a lovely spot by Mrs. Hudson, who came to see me the day after the burial and told me all about it.

"It was lovely, Mr. Holmes," Mrs. Hudson told me trying to hold back her tears, feeling obviously uncomfortable and awkward sitting upon the cot in my jail cell deep in the bowels of Scotland Yard. "They did a proper burial and nicely done ceremony. The Reverend Winslow officiated and he said many fine words concerning the Doctor."

I nodded.

"Well, I just thought you should know, that's all," she said softly, between sniffles. "And anyway, I also wanted to tell you something, Mr. Holmes. I been thinking about all that has happened. I want you to know that I do not hold it against you. What you did. You and the doctor had a terrible row, it got out of hand. I know you loved each other like brothers, and well, you know, brothers do get at each other sometimes. I have two brothers of me own and can tell you the truth of it. It's just so sad it got out of hand the way it did, that's all."

"I did not kill John, Mrs. Hudson," I told her firmly.

She nodded, but I could see she was merely placating me.

"I am serious. I did not kill him."

"Oh, come now, Mr. Holmes, I heard it all! I heard him with me own ears, I did! You and him arguing. The Doctor called out for you to stop, he cried out for you to put down the knife. He said your name, then cried out again and you... well... Then you stabbed him."

I looked at Mrs. Hudson closely, seriously, something was not right here. "Exact words now, please. Did he say put down the 'knife' or something else? Did he use some other word?"

Without hesitation she replied, "Why, he used the word 'knife,' I heard it clearly."

"Are you certain?"

"Of course. I know what I heard, Mr. Holmes. I told the police those very words."

"John was stabbed with my letter opener, *not* a knife," I told her.

I saw a spark of hope shine briefly in her eyes, then dark suspicion reasserted itself as before, "Oh, I don't know, a letter opener and a knife look pretty much alike to me."

"Yes, to you, but not to Watson," I stated sharply. "He saw me open my mail each morning with that very letter opener. Why did he not say the words 'letter opener' instead of 'knife'?"

"Well, I'm sure you're correct, Mr. Holmes," she admitted softly, but I could see she did not truly believe me. "It's just such a quibbling, tiny detail. It really means nothing at all."

"A small detail," I admitted sharply, "but it does mean something. Something small, something I may be missing."

She looked at me curiously and I saw the clouded look upon her face now.

"What is it?"

"Well, nothing really, but with all your talk about small and insignificant things, I remember one such that I forgot about but has now just occurred to me,"

"What is it?" I prompted eagerly. "Quickly, Mrs. Hudson, out with it!"

"Nothing really, just a feeling. I told you and the police I heard the doctor's voice, but I remember thinking at the time that I felt his voice was in a deeper tone, not quite like him at all. At the time I put it to the chaos of the situation, you know? I mean, after all, who else could it be but the doctor?"

"Who else, indeed, Mrs. Hudson," I smiled at her and she reluctantly smiled back.

"Well, Mr. Holmes I'll be going now. I just wanted to wish you the best in your upcoming trial. I have enjoyed having you and the doctor in my home these many years and I… Oh, Mr. Holmes, I miss him so much…"

"So do it."

She broke down in tears at that point, falling into my arms weeping openly for a moment. Then suddenly she recoiled from me as if in horror and stood up from the cot, looking at me closely and slowly moving away fearfully.

"Oh, no, you're the man who killed him! Poor Doctor Watson. I'm sorry, Mr. Holmes. I am so sorry. Guard! Guard, please take me out of here. Now!"

"Mrs. Hudson…"

"Goodbye, Mr. Holmes."

"I did not kill John, Mrs. Hudson."

Chapter 9
In Gaol

The days and nights in my prison cell slowly wore on. Mycroft's attorneys came in and did their utmost to prepare a strong defense but they told me the evidence was all against me. I am sure they had their own doubts as to my innocence. I'm afraid it was my fault as well, for I gave them awful little to work with. They saw my story about the Baron as a tangential matter that offered no real help to alleviate my current circumstances. I was not surprised by this, for I could see that Gruner had very neatly placed me into a deep fix in which there could be little hope of release.

My alibi of being at the Limehouse Pub during the time of the murder was also looked into once again by the police but with Shank Frobish dead and the pub burned down and in ruins now, no one there that night was talking. I was sure each of the denizens of the place had been paid off or threatened — or both — "take the money and keep yer mouth shut" was the message most likely and no one wanted to disobey it upon pain of death. There would be no help for me from that quarter and that alibi soon became a dead end. It was dropped from my case. None of the police believed any of it, even Lestrade thought it rather a lightweight story. There was no evidence for any of it, of course. Some of the critics in the press even went so far as to state that my so-called alibi seemed a very convenient made-up excuse to employ a dead man as a witness for my innocence. One critic stated that he expected better from someone of the stature of Sherlock Holmes!

The popular press continued to ramp up the scandal of Watson's murder and then my impending trial. One of the more vile aspects of the entire affair were press reports seemingly written by everyone who had a grudge against me — all being various criminals I had put behind bars. These 'worthies' came forward, of their own accord they said, and boldly spoke long and hard about how they had known all along that I was just a fake and that my methods were fraudulent.

What stung me was that their overriding message seemed to be that my 'so-called deductive methods' were nothing more than a sham, mere bunkum. Here again I saw the hand of Gruner orchestrating the situation from behind the scenes.

The high point — or low point, as you will notice in all this calumny — came to me the other morning. That is when Colonel Sebastian Moran, late of the old Moriarty gang, playing up his status as a military hero, no less — a man I long considered the second most dangerous man in London — broke his silence in an interview in the *Times*. There he spoke of how I used 'flim-flam' and 'tricks' to obtain dubious evidence that resulted in the conviction of many poor innocent men. Moran even went on to pen a short article for the newspaper entitled:

THAT SCOUNDREL, SHERLOCK HOLMES!
When I note the fact that this Sherlock Holmes — who murdered his best friend in cold blood, also murdered my own best friend — a terrible injustice has been done. I might add, that the fiend has never been brought to book for that murder, being the demise of the well-known scientist and beloved university professor, James Moriarty. Sherlock Holmes hounded that poor academic genius to his very grave, terrorizing a dear, sweet old professor who'd never harmed the hair on anyone's head. Why, the scoundrel Holmes, has even placed a taint upon my own fine reputation — and I, a military veteran and war hero! It's good to hear that Mr. Sherlock Holmes will finally get his just desserts. Good Riddance to him, I say. I shall be sure to be in attendance at the assizes for the hanging. I am sure the world will be a far better place without such a devil!

I threw the copy of the *Times* to the floor of my cell. Mycroft had left it with me, thinking I might be amused by the irony of it all. In fact, it made me rather sick. The situation seemed to be growing worse each day and just when I thought that it could get no worse, it did.

It was scant days before Shinwell "Porky" Johnson's scheduled execution. Then, the week after that, the murder trial of Sherlock Holmes was slated to begin. Things were as bleak as they'd ever been in my life and I desperately missed good old Watson each and every day that passed.

His good cheer, stout heart, fierce bravery and unquestioned loyalty were forever a boon to me in times of adversity — and now they were lost to me forever. His death left a void in my mind, my heart and my very soul.

"Oh, John," I sighed to myself before sleep one night, "I need you now. I miss you, old fellow."

My slumber that night was severely troubled and full of dark nightmarish images. I tossed and turned, then suddenly awoke with a start, my thoughts firmly fixed upon Shinwell Johnson of all people. It was two days before his execution and I'd not been able to speak with him since that first evening. The guards were under strict orders to keep the prisoners silent. They did not want things to get out of hand. I could understand that. I wasn't one for talking much myself those days in any case.

However, it wasn't the fact that Porky would be executed in two days that had startled me awake so sharply that night — as dire as that was — it was something that I remember him mentioning to me that first and only time we had been able to speak together. Something that had evidently connected deeply within my subconscious mind and was now swirling within my conscious mind. It was what he had said about the *type* of man Baron Gruner was, and the way the man's *mind* worked. And that got me thinking.

Gruner was a vile cunning beast, which was not in doubt, but he was also a supreme egoist and arrogant beyond all measure. That book he had compiled of his female conquests surely proved that his mind was a far darker pit, a more twisted sewer than ever I had considered. He had obviously not become more humble since Kitty's vitriol attack upon him three years ago. So now then, just what had he become?

If anything, I realized, the damage done to his face by Kitty had made Gruner a worse monster than he'd ever been, certainly more dangerous, more devious, but I was sure it had also unhinged his mind and that got me thinking. The Baron's plan had certainly been masterful. He'd planned well. He had murdered Kitty Winter to obtain his revenge upon her, then set up Porky for the crime, thereby getting his revenge upon Porky as well and in so doing send me this message that would set me up for what was to come. Now Porky rotted away in a cell down the hall from my own, as precious hours ticked away to the time of his execution. The Baron was well aware of all this. I was sure he was enjoying the knowledge of it, wherever he might be.

Next came his revenge against me. No — wait, not I specifically but against myself *and* good old Watson. The *two* of us. Which is something I am ashamed to admit that I had never fully considered in my own self-centered arrogance.

I thought back on it all and remembered that it had been Watson who had passed himself off at the Baron's residence as a seller of rare Chinese porcelain. Watson had gone to the Baron's home as I had instructed him to do, as part of my plan in the de Merville case. Watson was there during Kitty's attack upon Gruner. Watson had even used his doctoring skills to aid the Baron after the attack but to no avail, so deep had been the damage done. So Watson had been an integral part of this situation all on his own. He was not merely an adjunct to my own involvement, as I had first assumed.

I realized now that the Baron saw things differently from his point of view. His point of view was what was important here, not my own. I had missed that key fact in my arrogance and overwhelming conceit.

That had been my initial error, which I saw clearly now. Watson was one of the three principals who had been in the Baron's home that night when Gruner's disfigurement had been perpetuated by Kitty Winter.

I thought that over a bit more. I wished I had my pipe and tobacco. A good pipe always aided the thinking process. Nevertheless, I mulled this tack of thought over and wondered why I had not given it credence before. I can only put it down to my own blind arrogance mixed with my shock at the appearance of Watson's dead body lying on the floor of our rooms and the knowledge of his murder. A vision that haunts my every waking hour. I am afraid that my own emotionalism had also undone me, as much as the Baron's plan.

I was sure that he had counted on this from the onset of his plan.

In truth, I admit I had expected something of the sort from the Baron. But never this! He knew my feelings only too well and had played upon that knowledge creating certain assumptions for me in his plan, then I had allowed those assumptions to get the better of me. I chided myself harshly, remembering my axiom that where emotions are concerned, facts and evidence may not always be what they seem. Indeed! I heard the voice in my mind speak to me in alarm: *your eyes may not truly be seeing what you believe you are seeing!*

"Watson, old fellow, I know it now!" I said out loud, then I shouted boldly, "*I know it!*"

"*Hey, you, quiet down!*" a guard shouted at me from down the hall.

I just laughed.

Now I began to follow the thread of all this reasoning which lead me to the interesting possibility that Watson might *not* be dead after all. I looked at all that had transpired in a coldly logical manner, excising all emotion, then replacing it with the few hard facts I knew. Then I ran what I came up with into what I knew of the ways of Baron Gruner. It lead me to a new theory.

I had been truly devastated by the news of Watson's murder and the vision of his body upon the floor of our sitting room. I admit it; it had shocked me to the core. The vision left me reeling. So much so, that I was not thinking properly. I had too easily accepted what my eyes clearly showed me. I had noted the use of vitriol. I knew it was certainly another message to me from the Baron — instead of what it truly was — inspired misdirection. Of course, it had been nothing but a ruse. Lestrade saw its use merely as some vile way to torture poor Watson — in a manner to mutilate the body most disrespectfully. I had assumed the disfigurement as another message to me. And this is just what it appeared to be on the surface. However, deeper, underneath that surface, there was another reason for it's use, a much more sinister reason that I had missed.

Gruner had used vitriol upon Watson's body for one reason and one reason only. It was to cover the true identity of the body. Nothing more, nothing less. The Baron had played me for a fool since the beginning, capturing my emotions and using them for his own ends. First, he had used vitriol on Kitty's Winter's body — certainly for revenge — but the real reason was to pave the way for me to accept his use of it later, on Watson. Or the person he'd substituted for Watson. The Baron knew that I would accept what I saw then, and while repulsed by it, certainly not be surprised by it and even worse, not question it.

I had accepted it!

I had missed it all!

I idly wondered who the poor soul was whose body had been set in our rooms and dressed up as Watson. He had been wearing my friend's clothing, he even held Watson's father's prized watch in his hand.

The obvious question came to me immediately.

Where was the real Watson?

"How could I be so stupid!" I cried, my exasperation raged as the fire of the hunt seethed within me now. I pounded my fist upon the wall of my cell. I had finally figured it out!

Now what?

Watson and I had come up against the worst of criminals often enough in our many years of association. I thought of some of the worst now: the sinister Doctor Grimsby Roylott; the cunning Stapleton and his Hound of Hell at Baskerville Hall; then there was that vilest of blackmailers, Charles Augustus Malveton; and of course, the Napoleon of Crime himself, Professor James Moriarty — as well as his chief henchman, Colonel Sebastian Moran. All supremely dangerous men and all worthy criminal opponents. And yet, none of them rose to the level of the man I now found myself arrayed against. Now I must add Baron Adelbert Gruner to that list — and quite likely near the top. I had been such a fool. I had allowed assumptions driven by raw passion, wild emotions, and the sadness of a great all-consuming loss mixed with considerable guilt to interfere with my judgment and it had got the better of me. Just as it was intended to do.

I cried out, "Oh, John, will you ever forgive me!"

"Shut up!" the guard down the hall barked. *"Or I'll take a stick to you!"*

Chapter 10
The Plan

The next morning when Mycroft came to see me on his daily visit I laid it all out before him.

"Sherlock," my brother began softly, "I think it best you use your energies working with the barristers I have employed for your defense rather than indulge your remaining time and efforts in this...rather fanciful speculation. I admit it may have some merit, but...at this late date...we are severely pressed for time..."

"Then let us pursue it all the more in earnest," I said simply. "I have a plan."

Then I told him what I wanted to do.

"It will be difficult," my brother told me seriously, thinking it through, then nodding sagely. "I don't like it. It has some merit, but is risky. Lestrade will never go for it, I fear. But if you insist, I shall convince him. I will have to use all my powers to persuade him, but I shall try to do so."

"Then do so. He loses nothing either way it turns out. Impress upon him that fact. If we are successful then the Baron is undone. If not, I will turn myself in and the criminal case will proceed as before without interruption."

Mycroft shook his head. "I feel it is a risky gamble but I will support it with all my heart, Sherlock. I have had my man Morgan visit the home of the countess on two recent occasions and he has reported all normal there. I even had him report to you about his findings. You seemed to accept his report then, without comment."

"Yes, that is true, but I have been rather distracted of late..."

"No doubt and quite understandable."

"No, it is more than that. It was the Baron's plan for me all along. Listen,

Mycroft, when I questioned your man Morgan, I seem to remember he mentioned the individuals he noted in the routine of the countess. There were three older ladies related to her, a few local maids and household staff, but there were also four men. Butlers and grooms, no doubt, or said to be. One was even said to be her nephew whom Morgan never saw. The other three men were seen by him but he said they never spoke, even though Morgan told me he addressed them each personally. I believe they would not reply to him because to do so would have given up their Austrian accents. Those three men may not be German at all, but may in fact be Gruner's henchman. That nephew who was not seen, who was obviously in hiding at the time, must be Baron Gruner himself. He was hiding because his disfigurement would be easily noticed and surely give him away."

"You may be right," Mycroft said carefully. "However, Morgan is a good man and reported nothing amiss there."

"Perhaps, but I suspect the Baron is using the countess and her residence in Kent as a secret base of operations. The house and grounds are large enough to seclude him and a small group of henchmen, the dowager countess is so advanced in age and infirm she would hardly notice anything untoward going on in her own home. I am sure now that she offers the perfect cover for his schemes."

Mycroft nodded thoughtfully, "Very well, I will speak to Lestrade, and to his superiors. I will put it all unofficially, of course. You are still owed some favors in this country, Sherlock — as am I. I shall make this happen, but I can not vouch for the results. That shall remain on your head alone. Neither my people, nor Lestrade's representing the official police, can risk a raid upon the palace of the countess to seek out Baron Gruner without good cause. And we have none. She is highly connected and respected. Such an act would cause international scandal. But perhaps, one man, alone, might just pull off the deed."

"I'll not be alone, I'll have Porky with me," I told my brother with a smile.

"Ah, Shinwell Johnson, the professional criminal," Mycroft nodded in surprise. "Well, certainly, he may prove useful, if he has not been executed by then…"

Shinwell "Porky" Johnson sat alone in his jail cell below Scotland Yard counting the hours until he would be taken to the place where he would be hanged to the death for the murder of Kitty Winter, as well as the young aristocrat Simon Germaine. Two more innocents who had become caught in Baron Gruner's dark web of revenge.

Johnson knew his time was drawing near but he was surprised when he heard the key turn the lock on the cell block door down the hall. It was not yet dinner time, of that he was certain, so there was no reason for the guard to enter the block at this time. He listened intently and was further surprised to hear multiple voices speaking softly. Men were entering the block, the sound of their footsteps coming closer and closer to his cell. A sudden chill took him. Was it the execution squad? So soon?

Johnson waited patiently and eventually looked up to see a man leering down at him from the other side of the bars. Why, of all persons, he was surprised to find out that it was Inspector Lestrade himself! Beside the inspector he noticed a rather portly, well-dressed gentleman with intelligent piercing gray eyes that reminded Porky of his detective friend, Sherlock Holmes.

Lestrade motioned to the guard behind him, "Open his cell. Release him. Shinwell Johnson, you are ordered to follow me."

"Is it my time, so soon, Inspector?" Johnson asked nervously. Now that the hour was upon him he was amazed at how his fear had grown. "I thought I had another day or maybe even two before…you know? I guess I have lost track of time."

No one said a word. So Johnson just bowed his head and nervously followed the men down the corridor to his doom. They all walked in silence down the long corridor of the empty block until they reached my cell where his escort suddenly stopped. Johnson looked inside the cell and saw me in obvious surprise and relief.

"Mr. 'Olmes?" Johnson asked a mixture of curiosity and sadness in his voice. "It is good to see you one last time."

"It is not your last time, Porky," I told him and he looked at me dubiously.

"Guard, please unlock this door." Lestrade said stiffly, officiously. "Mr. Sherlock Holmes, please exit your cell now."

I got up from my cot and did as I was told. I noticed Mycroft give me a sly wink. I nodded back with a grim little smile; the old dog had pulled it off! He had convinced Lestrade and the Yard to go along with my plan! Lestrade looked as dour as usual but that was to be expected from such a by-the-book fellow. Meanwhile, I saw an incredulous look of hope growing on Shinwell Johnson's face.

Lestrade looked over to the guard, "All right, Tidwell, that will be all for now. You are to report to Sergeant Jones upstairs immediately. Under no circumstances are you to ever speak of anything you have seen or witnessed here tonight. Do I make myself clear? Or I swear I shall have the hide off you!"

"Yes, sir!" Tidwell saluted smartly and was soon gone.

"Well, let's go, Mr. Holmes — and you too, Johnson," Lestrade ordered. "You don't have a lot of time."

"Thank you, Lestrade," I said as we walked down the cell block.

"Thank your brother, he made me see the light — whether I wanted to do so or not! He can be most persuasive, even forceful. I don't like breaking the rules, Mr. Holmes, which you seem to have taken a particular delight in doing during your career, but I am not unaffected by the murder of Doctor Watson, as well as your own plight. I only did my job, going where the evidence took me."

"I understand fully."

"No, I do not think you do, Mr. Holmes. I am a Scotland Yard detective. I have given my oath to serve the law and punish the guilty. But I admit that I can make a mistake as well as the next man. You see, I was mightily shocked by the doctor's murder. I tell you it threw me for a loop at first and I was most fiercely angry with you about it. However, afterwards, when I thought about it more deeply, I was sure you could never have done such a thing. Most unlikely of you, I say. Of course all the evidence was there, so it seemed quite clear, but even with that, it all appeared just a bit too pat for this old inspector to swallow. Dare I say it? In a corner of my mind it appeared as if it were all somehow artificially contrived. Perhaps, even as you say? I recalled your words about the Baron, then thought again of Watson's murder. Damn impossible that you could do such a thing, I see that now, if I may be so bold. Which meant I had a big problem. I had an innocent man in my jail cell — while the true killer was out free. I tell you true, that rankles any true blue copper as nothing else can. So when your brother came to me with this scheme — and believe me I knew that it could be the end of my career, a career by the way that I in large part owe to you and the doctor on numerous occasions — I decided to acquiesce to his suggestion. Not to mention his considerable political pressure from on high."

"I see, Lestrade," I said with genuine gratitude. "Nevertheless I thank you, if for nothing else than for being such a fine officer of the law who seeks the true killer in this case and will allow me to bring him to book."

Lestrade actually allowed a wan smile to flit across his face at my compliment. "We'll see how long I remain at the Yard, unless you are successful, Mr. Holmes. Come now, there are a few rules you need to know about."

"Rules?" I blurted.

Mycroft looked at me and Johnson with serious concern, "This is how we shall play this particular game, gentlemen. If Doctor Watson is alive, you need to find him before Baron Gruner or his men can dispatch him. For Watson is your only witness, he can corroborate this entire affair and clear you both. We know now that the man buried in Watson's gave was *not* the doctor. After some reluctance from the family I arranged an exhumation of the grave yesterday."

"Mycroft!" I blurted my surprise all too evident that my brother had never let on to me about his undercover activities upon my behalf. "You never fail to amaze me."

"Ah, Sherlock, you above all others should know the Service never sleeps. We cover all bases, but I thought it best to keep things mum until I discovered definite facts that could be of use to us."

I nodded, "And what did you discover?"

Mycroft gave me a wry grin, "While the man in Watson's grave *appeared* to be the doctor in size and form, right on down to that old military scar apparently the result of a Jezzial bullet — remember his face had been conveniently destroyed by the vitriol — we decided to try a new tack."

"Dental records?" I surmised. I had heard such records were newly in use back then in some cases, but many courts still did not accept them. Nevertheless, it offered enough doubt of the identity of the man in that grave for our purposes.

Mycroft nodded, "Right you are, and they showed us some interesting discrepancies. The body from the grave seemed to have grown back two molars that Watson's dental records clearly show us had been removed from the doctor's mouth last year."

"I well remember the grand toothache it gave him," I laughed lightly, allowing a deep sigh of relief. "So it is conclusive now. That body was *not* Watson's."

"It was not him, but have a care, Sherlock. It only proves the man found dead in your flat was not Dr. Watson, it does not prove you did not kill him," Mycroft cautioned, adding sharply, "nor that Watson may still be alive."

I nodded in grim realization of my brother's wise words.

"Then what about Kitty?" Johnson asked eagerly now, his face showing a thin thread of hope. "Could the same apply to her as well, Sir?"

Here Mycroft frowned sadly, placing his hand upon the man's shoulder in a gesture of stalwart support and fellowship that he rarely evidenced, "No, I am afraid not. I am sorry."

Johnson nodded tersely, he had expected as much. Then he looked at me, "Well, at least the doctor may still be alive."

"He is alive, I know it!" I said with renewed hope and vigor.

I saw Porky nodding his head in agreement, and even dour Lestrade's face seemed to brighten with hope now. Obviously Mycroft's news of the discovery made in Watson's dental records had been told to the inspector earlier, even as it had been unknown to Johnson and myself until this moment.

Mycroft warned carefully, "You will be engaged in a tricky maneuver here, gentlemen. Even should you find the Baron, he is not wanted for any crimes in this country. He can not be arrested or even held without compelling evidence. Watson is that evidence. Remember, should you fail in this scheme, his connections and the scandal of a raid by the police would cause a firestorm to come down on all our heads. We have just discovered that Alexa von Huenfeld, the dowager countess, is in fact, the German Kaiser's older sister. That means she is not only related to the German royal family, but through those connections, to our own good King Edward himself."

Well that certainly put a new complexion on things and we were all silent for a moment absorbing the implications. I looked tensely at my brother, I had not known this fact, but I now realized Baron Gruner's connections ran quite high indeed.

"Sherlock, you will have to infiltrate the estate under cover. Take Mr. Johnson with you. Try to find Watson and free him. He may be held as a prisoner — or he may already be dead. I am sorry to say it, but I must be blunt, it may be true. If the latter be the case, try to find his body, that will also be useful as evidence — its discovery will raise questions useful in your defense."

"I am sure Watson is alive," I said confidently.

"He may not be, Mr. Holmes," Lestrade added carefully, "so while you hope for the best, do prepare yourself for the worst."

"I can not believe the Divine Providence that has been with me all my life has lead me down this long and nightmarish road only to reward me with the death of my good friend at the very end of my path," I said with bold confidence now. "No, I am sure that can not be the case. Watson is alive and I shall find him. Now, let's get on with it!"

Lestrade spoke up then, explaining for Porky's benefit rather than my own: "You both are to break into the estate of the countess. Once you free Watson, or discover his body, give me the signal and I will have my men rush in to aid you. If you do not find Watson, I must hold my men back. That is the best that I can offer under the present circumstances."

"Politics!" Johnson spat with contempt.

"Politics is what has got you out of gaol, my good man, and it has given you this last chance," Mycroft told Johnson sharply. "So I suggest you make the most of it."

"You both have done more than enough," I told the Inspector and my brother.

Porky nodded, "Sure as I do appreciate it, sirs, I meant no disrespect. This last chance you have given me to avenge me poor wee Kitty is precious to me."

Lestrade nodded grimly, "Then use it well."

"Now be careful and work fast," Mycroft instructed us. "You only have a few hours to pull this off. If you bollocks it up, the story will be put forward that you escaped from Scotland Yard and that Lestrade apprehended you outside the estate of the Countess Von Huenfeld. We must avert scandal at all costs."

I nodded, looking from Mycroft to Lestrade, ready to be off.

"Then here are your train tickets," Mycroft said handing me an envelope. "There is a cab standing by to take you straight away to Waterloo Station. From there you can be in Kent in two hours, hire a trap, and enter the grounds of the palace of the countess before midnight. Make the most of your time, gentlemen, events are moving rapidly. If you discover anything give the signal, Lestrade and his men will be looking out for it. Without that signal, I am afraid Lestrade will not be able to act."

"We understand," I told my brother, looking over to Johnson, who nodded with grim determination.

"Good luck, Sherlock, and to you also, Mr. Johnson." Then we all shook hands and said our goodbyes. Looking at Porky, Mycroft asked, "Please watch out for my little brother, will you, Mr. Johnson?"

"Aye, Mr. Mycroft, I'll guard him with me life, I will. You can depend on Porky."

"Well come now, Porky, let us be off. We have a Baron to track down and we have to save the life of Doctor Watson before it is too late. The game is afoot!"

"Well come now, Porky, let us be off. We have a Baron to track down and we have to save the life of Doctor Watson before it is too late. The game is afoot!"

Chapter 11
The Man in The Cage

In a secluded estate my long-lost friend Doctor John Watson was being held prisoner. Here is his story, just as he told it to me.

When I awoke I found myself in a small cage or cell made of stout iron bars on all fours sides. The cage was located in the center of a large drawing room, obviously in some palatial building that seemed to be in a somewhat dilapidated or unused state. I found myself alone. There was total silence. The huge room was unattended and the far away doors I could see at both ends of the room were shut.

What had happened to me?

My head throbbed as I tried to remember. It came back to me slowly. I must have been hit from behind, rather hard. There was dried blood and a memorable lump upon my head that hurt like the dickens. I sat upright and then it all came flooding back to me.

The Baron!

Mycroft's visit had ended, Holmes had then retired to his room, and I was left alone in our sitting room at Baker Street.

Time passed. Mrs. Hudson brought up our dinner. Holmes was still ensconced in his room so I knocked upon his bedroom door to get his attention but I received no response. Being well aware of how my companion could become once he was hot upon a case — and specifically this one where his very life was in peril — I pleaded with my friend outside his closed door to open up and come out, to eat some dinner in an effort to keep up his strength. I knew that he must allow his body and mind much needed sustenance.

Holmes never answered my pleas, or my knocking.

Finally I tried his door, and finding it unlocked, turned the knob. Upon entering the room I was surprised to discover that Sherlock Holmes was gone. The back window was opened a crack and a gentle breeze filtered through the room, but the Great Detective was nowhere to be seen.

I looked over at the empty bed; it had not even been slept in. Then I looked over the rest of the empty room and wondered where Holmes was and what he was doing. I sighed deeply, now what was I to do?

Stay here and hold down the fort, old man, I said to myself mimicking my friend's voice in my mind. *I will be back soon enough and have some good news that will break this case wide open!*

I slowly walked out of my friend's empty bedroom wrapped in my own bleak thoughts; absently I entered our sitting room. I froze with sudden terror at what I saw there.

"Doctor Watson, I presume?" a deep voice toned menacingly from behind a dark facial mask worn by a tall, shrouded man. He stood boldly in our sitting room, a dark visage, a fearful image. "It appears we meet again!"

The intruder was ensconced in darkness, a bleak black robe, covering similar clothing that was also as dark as night, and he wore a sinister facial mask that covered all his features quite effectively, but that appeared as twisted and bleak as some vision from deepest darkest hell itself.

"You!" I whispered dreadfully.

The man did not say another word but he carefully took off his bizarre mask to show me his true face — or the lack of it. I tell you in all candor seeing his actual face put the fear of death into me straight away. What was left of that face appeared to be an evil vision from beyond the grave itself; something created by rotting corruption and molded with melted flesh. I was horrified and gasped in spite of my vast medical experience, going so far as to take an involuntary step backwards in utter revulsion. I'd worked on burn victims and seen lepers in India with less traumatic damage to their faces than this fellow. That face was haunting; it could not help but instill a deep fear and loathing within anyone who saw it. I had surely never seen the likes before. Or had I?

Of course I realized instantly now who the man before me was. It was the very man Sherlock Holmes had half of London searching for — Baron Adelbert Gruner!

"So I see, you recognize me," my intruder said with a menacing growl and for the first time I noticed the weapon in his hand that was aimed at my heart. Silently he motioned me to fully enter the sitting room and take a seat.

"What do you want?" I demanded boldly.

"To talk. That is all, for now," he told me simply, and for a brief moment I hoped that I might be able to reason with the man. He had to know he was being eagerly sought out. Perhaps I could trade him his freedom and safe exit from England, if he just dropped his plans of revenge against Holmes, and cleared Shinwell Johnson of murder.

But I saw it was not to be. The man's evil nature had massively asserted itself ever since the incidence of his physical destruction three years before. The Baron had then been an extraordinarily handsome gentleman, a man of high breeding and great wealth whose rugged good looks and charm made women swoon with delight and crave his every attentions; women such as the young and impressionable Violet de Melville. But now his outside camouflaging shell of attractiveness and charm had been swept away by his injury and all that remained was the vile pustular disfigurement that mirrored the man's true inner nature. The actual ugliness and evil of the man that was there inside him, was now shown plainly on the outside as well. It was ghastly.

I suddenly became fearful of my life.

"So I suppose you are going to kill me?" I asked, refusing to take a seat, figuring that come what may, I would hold my ground boldly in front of his weapon, his anger. "Do what you will, Baron. Seek your twisted version of revenge. It is of no matter, for Sherlock Holmes will surely avenge me. He will see to it that you will swing in the dock for my murder."

The Baron laughed mockingly, "Sherlock Holmes? Sherlock Holmes is dead."

I froze with a monstrous chill of dread at the very word. Dead? Sherlock Holmes? It could not be! I hardly knew how to respond, I was so shocked, stunned, dismayed. My good friend, Sherlock Holmes, dead?

Or was the Baron just playing with me? Mocking me? I looked at him sharply. Defiant. "I do not believe you."

"It is true. My men caught him alone and unawares, they killed him bare hours ago."

"You bastard!" I whispered in dreadful shock. My God, Sherlock Holmes, dead? I would not allow myself to believe it, and yet…

Baron Gruner laughed, he was obviously vastly entertained by my reaction to his news, then he carefully placed the mask back upon his face. It was then that I noticed there was another man in the room with him. He was an enormous fellow and he stood in front of a large trunk. I sighed dejectedly, ready to accept what was to come, I was outnumbered and outgunned.

"Well go ahead. Do it!" I stated sharply, standing firmly defiant to the end. "Shoot! Kill me! I do not care any longer. Just get it over with."

The Baron just laughed at me, "Oh, I will not kill you, Doctor Watson. Not now, not yet. Though before I am through with you, I assure you that you will wish I had shot you dead right here this very second."

I took a deep breath, my words had been bold but I was shaking with fear and trepidation. I closed my eyes thinking of Holmes, and despite the Baron's words I awaited the gun shot that I was sure would end my life.

It never came.

I opened my eyes and looked once again at the Baron. He began to laugh at me showing great joy. It was an evil joy brought out by his sinister plans and it shook him so deeply it was horrible to see.

"I am afraid, Doctor, it will not be quite so easy."

Then I felt a blow to the head, and I sank down to the floor unconscious.

Now I was alone in a cell ruminating over my predicament. I recalled the Baron held a weapon on me. Why had he not used it? Then I thought about Holmes. Not only was he missing, but a fearful shiver hit me when I recalled the Baron had told me the Great Detective was dead. I froze at the very though of Sherlock Holmes' death. It could not be! It must not be! My heart and soul ached at the very thought. I could not believe it.

I refused to believe it! Then an inspired thought came to me. Why would the Baron hold me here, alive — why keep me alive at all — if Holmes were dead?

I whispered forcefully, "I know that you are alive and I know that you will come for me, Holmes. I just know it!"

I sat down upon the cot in my cage and considered my plight.

The Baron had caused all this. I knew he was doing it for revenge, but just what form was that revenge taking? Well, I knew my questions would be answered soon enough once Baron Gruner came to confront me. For I knew the man's monstrous ego could never allow him to miss the opportunity to mock me and gloat over the power he now held over me as his prisoner. At the time I had no idea what form, nor how devious, that revenge had taken.

It all began the next morning when I was startled by the opening of the large French doors at the far end of the room and in walked Baron Adelbert Gruner himself, along with one of his henchmen.

The Baron still wore the gruesome mask that I remember had covered his face when I had first encountered him in our sitting room at Baker Street. That had been a night or two ago I imagine, but I could not tell for certain, for I had lost all track of time here. I could see his mask better now in the daylight. It was a truly hideous visage, melted and twisted in such a manner so as to make him appear to be a mad man. Perhaps he was. Why would any man seek to wear such a thing?

"Doctor Watson," Baron Gruner said with mocking good cheer, "so good of you to visit me."

"What have you done? Release me immediately!" I demanded.

Baron Gruner just laughed at my bold order, then nodded, "Of course, I shall release you, Doctor, but all in good time. For now, I want you to be my guest, enjoy my hospitality, and be a witness to my...revenge. Know this; all the world believes you to be dead now — murdered by your best friend, Sherlock Holmes!"

I looked at him sharply, surprised — actually astounded by what he had just told me.

"That's... that is preposterous! No one would ever believe such a thing."

"Oh, I assure you, it is true, Doctor. You see my plan has worked magnificently."

"Your plan! No! No, that can not be!" I shouted, shocked by his devilish words. I saw the contradiction in those words immediately and it gave me some slim measure of hope. I looked into his eyes and told him boldly, "Then what of Holmes? So you admit he is not dead as you first told me? He still lives!"

The Baron just laughed in grim joy, loud dark mirth mixed with evil menace, "Yes, he is alive...for now. I must admit it, I lied when I told you my men had killed him. It was a tiny conceit of mine that I could not resist when I first confronted you. I hope you can forgive me? Oh, but it was so entertaining. You should have seen the look upon your face at the news, the shock, and the pain! It was simply priceless! I could not resist. I do apologize."

The man must be mad!

My eyes shot him a look of fierce anger, "You are a vile beast!"

Baron Gruner only laughed the more at these words, wild with pleasure, obviously enjoying this mocking confrontation, and my feelings of abject helplessness. Finally he motioned to the large man standing behind him, "Sergey, you may present the Doctor with the newspapers."

Then Baron Gruner's henchman, who was a giant of a man with cold, cruel eyes and black teeth, approached my cell and threw various newspapers to me between the bars. I saw that they were the London *Times* and other daily papers.

"Read all about it, Doctor Watson." The Baron mocked in stinging words. "It makes for fascinating news.“

He laughed wildly as he and his henchman, Sergey, walked out of the room leaving me alone.

Once Gruner and his man were gone I picked up the newspapers and looked them over carefully. They appeared to be genuine. In the pile were included most of the major London dailies, the popular press as Holmes was fond of calling them, and each one seemed to blare headlines fixated on the latest London scandal — the murder of Doctor Watson by his friend, Sherlock Holmes!

I was aghast as I looked over the various headlines.

One shouted at me in bold type:

IS THIS THE END OF SHERLOCK HOLMES?

Another proclaimed with sensationalistic alarm:

WATSON MURDERED, HOLMES IN CUSTODY!

I read them, and as I read I shook with rage and shock at what Baron Gruner had wrought. For surely he was responsible for all this. It was terrible. It could not be true! And yet it was true! The very knowledge cut me to the core of my being, just as he had planned, no doubt.

I wondered; did Holmes know the truth? Did he have an inkling that I was really alive and being held as a prisoner of the Baron? What I read in the papers about it all seemed to indicate otherwise. I read over each newspaper very carefully, three times. Not only reading the printed words themselves but trying my best to gauge what information I could glean from what was written as Holmes would often say, "between the lines" — what was *not* said. Also by *how* things were being said. It was one of the many methods I had picked up from my close association with Holmes those many years.

What I found out only caused me to sink into despair. Things looked dire for Holmes, all the evidence indicated he had murdered me in cold blood, and the press and the people seemed to have turned against him. There were calls for his death. I shuddered in fear for my friend.

I read on, learning more, and it fairly drove me mad. Here I was locked away in an iron-barred cell in absolute seclusion while my best friend and the best man I had ever known had been arrested as the person responsible for my murder.

I read how Holmes had been charged and was now in custody in a cell in Scotland Yard. I shook in rage and anger at all Baron Gruner had caused. Little did I realize that first day the length and extent of the man's wickedness. Little did I imagine then, the horrific plan of his ultimate revenge.

The Baron visited me each morning to inform me of the latest progress of the case against Holmes as reported in the daily papers. I usually did not engage him on these matters, but it only caused him to laugh the harder as he mocked me with joyful abandon. I realized the man could not deny himself the pleasure of taunting me, mocking me, as he openly shared with me the latest bit of ugly gossip about the brutal scandal.

"How it must rankle you, Doctor, to be locked away here, when your friend is accused of your murder," Baron Gruner prompted with sardonic humor. "Ironic, is it not? If only you were free! Then you could go to Scotland Yard and clear this all up immediately. But of course, you are not free. What a shame."

I did not reply. I did not want to give the man the satisfaction. However one troubling bit of evidence was preying upon my mind.

"What about the body?" I asked him. "Who was the poor unfortunate you passed off as me? How did you manage this all with a man on guard outside our building?"

"Ah, yes, the impostor and the guard outside your building," Gruner nodded his head in mock seriousness, but I knew he was grinning at me in mockery behind his mask. "A man of no consequence who fit your measurements exactly, right down to a similar wound from his military service."

"A military man and you murdered him!"

"I imagine he was formerly of the military, but he did prove useful," Gruner told me simply, without any feeling, showing me all too clearly he was an evil brute. I told him so exactly. He ignored my words then added ominously, "Better you should ask me about the vitriol."

"Yes, what of it?" I asked.

"The vitriol was my calling card used explicitly to gain the attention of your friend, Mr. Holmes. I know that after I had used the vitriol on that whore, Kitty Winter, Holmes could not fail to see the connection. My calling card and a message directly to Holmes. I knew his arrogance, his conceit, once mixed with his emotions from your murder would blind him to what I had truly done. His assumptions would do the rest. In his supreme arrogance, being the confident know-it-all that he is, Sherlock Holmes would miss the actual reason for the use of the vitriol in the first place."

"What are you saying?" I blurted.

"I used the acid not for revenge as it so obviously appeared — but to destroy the face of the man who was made up to be you, Doctor. It was done to obscure identification. For that reason only. I knew Sherlock Holmes would be utterly shocked by your murder, horrified by what had been done to the corpse, no doubt he felt responsible for leaving you alone, awash in guilt, as he most certainly should! I counted on that to cause him to miss a crucial piece of the puzzle. I fooled him quite nicely."

I hardly knew how to respond to his words but I suddenly became very fearful for Holmes, feeling the tight noose of an all encompassing doom grow firmly about us both.

"Nothing to say, Doctor?" the Baron taunted.

"You shall pay for this!"

The Baron just laughed.

This was not working, but I wanted to keep him talking. I changed the subject. "What of the man stationed outside 221 and the men at both ends of Baker Street? How did you elude them?"

The Baron seemed to enjoy explaining his success, showing off the brilliance of his plan, which I had to admit, seemed to be working perfectly. "That was nothing; a mere distraction in the street. Then me and my man, Sergey, being dressed as workmen, carried the body of your impostor into the building in a trunk that we were delivering. We had all the time we needed once in your rooms to set up the murder scene. Then Sergey and I took you out of the building in the very same trunk."

"What of Mrs. Hudson?" I blurted.

"Yes, such a trusting and naive woman. She helped me pull it all off right before her eyes, and ears, with no one the wiser."

"You seem to have thought of everything?" I stammered glumly.

"It was quite a detailed plan but well constructed. I had put many months of work into it to ensure success," the Baron said proudly. "There could be no other result."

"So what now?" I asked bitterly, marveling in spite of myself, at the insane genius of the man.

"For now, you are my guest. You are here to observe, to watch, to enjoy. Each morning you will be presented with the London newspapers so you may keep up to date with the Sherlock Holmes murder case. After all, you are one of the principals and intimately involved. Savor it, Doctor Watson. The popular press has positively become rabid with the growing scandal. Some of the most imaginative writing by your Fleet Street scribes has appeared in these rags, and I tell you in all modesty, it makes for vastly entertaining reading — even if not entirely accurate. Then there is the coming murder trial. I am assured it will begin in a few weeks, which I am sure will offer further scandal and eventually result in the rope for Mr. Sherlock Holmes."

"No! That shall never happen!"

"Oh, yes, it shall all come to pass, mark my words. Everything is nicely planned and moving along smoothly. Holmes is doomed — and so, my good doctor — are you! After his execution, you will be taken to a place of concealment, shot and buried in an unmarked grave. And none will be the wiser. But first, I want you to experience first hand, his doom and utter destruction."

My face blanched with dread. Baron Gruner could see my reaction and was buoyed by it.

"Does all this upset you, Doctor Watson? Does it strike you hard and fast with the unfairness of it all, the absolute cunning, and the very touch of sheer genius behind it?" Baron Gruner mocked.

"You are a devil! A monster! You will drive me mad! Is that what you want to do, to drive me mad?" I shouted in rage. I had lost all control, anger and frustration clouded my mind by the sheer shock of all I had been told. And poor Holmes all alone, believing me dead, suffering so gravely no doubt with the full import of that knowledge, and I am sure with much unwarranted guilt. It was just too much to contemplate.

"That is good, Doctor. I am gratified to see such a reaction," Baron Gruner laughed wildly in satisfaction as he blithely walked out of the room.

This torment went on for days. Baron Gruner would come in each morning to mock me, while one of his lackeys would slip that morning's newspapers to me between the bars of my cell. I was not physically abused, but I did not need to be, for the mental torment was by far enough. I was given three meals each day, but never allowed to leave my cell for any reason. Not even for the necessities of hygiene for which I was allowed a simple bucket of water and bedpan. It seemed I was locked away in that cage for good, secure and helpless. I feared the effect was slowly unhinging my senses.

I believe the newspapers were the worst part of it all. I could not bring myself to look at them but I could not look away. The lies that were written so boldly, the scandal and the public outcry against Holmes were simply atrocious.

I even read of my own funeral, pitying the poor soul who Baron Gruner had used in my place, a man who now rested in my own casket, in my very own grave. Next to my own dearly departed Mary. It was an outrage!

And all orchestrated by Baron Gruner.

The popular press presented the most outrageous fabrications of the crime with all manner of dark implications and gruesome details. They lingered on the use of the vitriol; calling for the noose for Holmes because they said what he had done not only mocked the dead but had desecrated my body. The use of the acid went over badly with the public and put Holmes in a sinister light. Fleet Street scribes also lingered upon the six stab wounds, going on endlessly about the animal rage of my friend. They wrote incessantly of how my helpless pleas for life had been heard by our poor old landlady. That I had pleaded with Holmes for my life, but he had ruthlessly murdered me in a wild rage of cold blood. It was despicable and they focused on every gory detail, often lingering in their descriptions upon the blood and gore.

One such daily publication even implied that my murder by Holmes had been because of some kind of …some kind of unnatural…dalliance! Utter rubbish! Foul lies! Yet the press persisted in presenting these rumors, vile innuendos, and even outright lies, as the truth. No doubt much of this was presented to them through agencies of the Baron.

What was I to do?

I realized that there was nothing that I could do.

I did try to escape.

Early on I had tried a bold escape ruse, apparently fainting in front of the Baron's man, remaining motionless. Baron Gruner had been summoned yet was unaffected by my little game.

When one of his men spoke up that I might be ill, or even dying, the Baron simply said, "So be it. My orders are that no one opens his cell under any conditon. I have the only key and I do not care if he dies."

My rations were cut the next day because of this failed and inept attempt and Baron Gruner only laughed about it later, impressing upon me that I was quite neatly trapped like a rat and that there was nothing I could do about it.

I began to think he might be right.

It sickened me as I continued to read more regarding my friend Sherlock Holmes and the dire predicament he now found himself in. My soul ached at what he must be going through, not only with my supposed death, but with all the scandal attached to it. Sherlock Holmes' brilliant reputation was being sullied day by day and Baron Gruner made sure that I was given the newspapers each day to follow every word; every accusation.

After a week of this horror I vowed not to ever look at the newspapers the Baron's henchman handed to me each morning, but I found I could not ignore them. As horrid as they were, as full of lies as they might be, I yearned for any news of my friend, and of his plight. It was difficult, maddening to my senses, and of course Baron Gruner had planned it all to have just that effect.

I read of the barristers Holmes had employed to plead his cause, all good men, but the case was said to be open and shut by those in the know. The evidence was said to be striking. I read where blood had been found in Holmes' room; his own letter opener had apparently been used as the murder weapon; and none other than our good and trusted landlady, Mrs. Hudson, had admitted to the police that she had heard it all from her kitchen downstairs. She had told of hearing me beg Holmes to put down the knife.

I read where our loyal landlady told of hearing my last words, which had been plastered boldly on one newspaper's front page:

DOCTOR WATSON'S LAST WORDS —
"PLEASE SHERLOCK, DON'T KILL ME!"

Then the article went on in endless gory detail about how he had continued to stab me time and time again, until I died.

"Poppycock!" I barked angry, albeit grimly aware of the cold facts that Holmes was up against. Why they'd even tricked good old Mrs. Hudson!

I sighed deeply, it appeared all was lost and I feared more than ever for my friend.

The days of my captivity wore on. They were long and uneventful, except for Baron Gruner's daily visits to mock me and the time I spent reading the trash in the popular press. I soon understood Holmes' disdain for newspapers and what went for journalism in London. The days wore on, long and dark.

I did follow other bits of news reported in the press, especially the case of Shinwell "Porky" Johnson, who was scheduled to be executed in a couple of days for the murder of Kitty Winter and the young man who had hired her for a few hours of mindless pleasure. Two innocents in the Baron's gruesome death tally — and soon Porky Johnson as well.

There was never any good news I could see, and hope seemed to slip away from me and evaporate as the days wore on.

My nights were fraught with fear and sadness for my friend. It was maddening to think of what he must be going through.

He had failed.

I had failed.

I had failed him.

I was having trouble sleeping, I could not get the terror of all this out of my mind, even for a moment.

I am not ashamed to say that I cried often, wracking sobs of helplessness and utter despair at the Baron's victory over us. Such a terrible injustice could not be made to stand but I knew the dire truth that stared me in the face, so I no longer held any hope. So many lives had been ruined by that man. And soon another, Shinwell Johnson, another innocent, would die upon the gallows. No doubt, after the trial, Holmes would follow him to the rope. Then being of no further use, I would be taken out and discreetly taken care of, but only after Baron Gruner had extracted his last ounce of pleasure from the pus of my bile.

Only then would Baron Adelbert Gruner be completely victorious and the name of Sherlock Holmes, and all that he stood for, be forever linked with scandal and murder. Holmes' name and once heroic career would be degraded in deep shame. I tell you the very thought of it caused my blood to boil. A man who stood for nothing but goodness and justice throughout his life was being devilishly wronged. It galled me terribly. I screamed in rage at the sheer injustice of it. However, no one heard my pleas, not even Baron Gruner. I sat alone in my cage, day after day, powerless to stop it all, angry with useless fury.

I feared I was slowly losing my faculties.

I do not know how long I had been indisposed in black despair but at some point I suddenly noticed that Baron Gruner was standing before my cell quietly appraising me like I was some exhibit at the Hyde Park Zoo. Or in his own hellish personal zoo?

"That's very good, Doctor," he said with evident pleasure. "I am gratified to see that the full impact of my plan finally has touched you down to your very soul."

"You shall be made to pay for all your deeds!" I shouted, trying to remain defiant.

The Baron just laughed at my feeble response, "Really? And pray tell who shall make me pay? You, Doctor Watson? No one knows you are even here. Sherlock Holmes? I'm afraid he is rather occupied at the moment. No, you must face the facts; there is no one to save you…or him."

"You will pay! Sherlock Holmes will find a way!" I cried, with a confidence I surely did not feel at the time.

The Baron laughed wildly with a long and deeply joyous mirth that was supremely mocking in the depth of its hatred.

I fear I lost it then. I began screaming the foulest expletives at him, but he hardly seemed to notice my words at all. His attention appeared to be off in some other realm of reality, apparently starring off into the distance, far away from me for the moment, locked in his own twisted

At some point I suddenly noticed that Baron Gruner was standing before my cell quietly appraising me like I was some exhibit at the Zoo.

world. I realized then that the man was utterly insane.

Baron Gruner's attention came back to my world eventually, his mind back to present reality. He looked down at me and threw another newspaper into my cell. "Here, read this! The comments by the Colonel on the front page should inspire you further."

Then he left me, his mocking laughter echoing in that huge room until he was gone. I could still hear his muffled voice from the other side of the door as he closed it behind him and walked away.

I found myself alone once again.

I sat down and tried to get control of my raging emotions. I realized I had to think this through logically, keep my senses intact, and somehow escape this cell. I had to find a way to freedom and then bring this all to the attention of Scotland Yard.

I had to clear Holmes, and if I could, before it was too late, save Shinwell Johnson. Time was running out. I tried to come up with a scheme, any scheme, but there appeared no way out of this locked iron cage and no way the Baron would allow the door to be opened.

I sat down hopelessly and wept.

I read the article on the front page of one of the more prestigious dailies regarding Colonel Sebastian Moran's comments about Holmes and his situation. A more self-serving pack of lies by a loathsome criminal about the Great Detective has never been written. I tell you, it got my blood boiling. But what was I to do about it?

One of the Baron's men brought me food three times a day. It was accomplished without any physical contact. I had tried on numerous occasions to engage the man in conversation but he would not respond. The man had been trained well and instructed not to speak to me for any reason whatsoever, or venture close enough to the bars for me to come at him. He kept well away from me. Not that it mattered anyway, none of the Baron's men had a key to my cage, there was only one key and the Baron himself had it.

I wracked my brains every hour of every day to come up with some scheme to get that key, but it was all to no avail. It seemed Baron Gruner had thought of everything.

I tried to pick the lock time and time again as well, but it proved impossible for me. Perhaps a locksmith, or Holmes himself, might have been able to best it given enough time, but it was far beyond my meager capabilities.

So that left me alone, feeling suffocated by bleak despair, a prisoner in my cage, wasting the few days I had left, while precious time ticked away for my friend, Sherlock Holmes. I raged at the execution of Shinwell Johnson scheduled, the papers told me, for just a day or two away. I raged at what Baron Gruner had caused to come to pass. His revenge was as cunning and diabolical a thing as I had ever though possible. It caused me unimaginable terror and torment.

I feared we were doomed.

Chapter 12
Mr. Holmes and Mr. Johnson

"*Y*ou know I am with you all the way, Mr. 'Olmes."

"Hurry now, Porky, we have little time," I told my companion as we exited the train at the station in Kent and quickly hired a trap to take us to the palace of the Dowager Countess Alexa Von Huenfeld.

Inspector Lestrade and his men from Scotland Yard were following behind, but not too closely, so as not to arouse suspicion. Depending on what we discovered, they would act accordingly.

"I am sure that the doctor is still alive," Porky told me as our driver took us into the lovely Kentish countryside, so overflowing with greenery and flowers that it is often referred to as the Garden of England, but this dark night it felt sinister to me as we rode towards the estate the countess had rented.

"I admit I am not entirely positive that Watson is still alive, Porky," I cautioned, not daring to allow my words to soar with false hope. "The Baron is a complicated man. He may have abducted John and then killed him straight away in some different location, or may yet be holding him so he could do him in at his leisure. Or, God forbid, torture him. Gruner is an altogether vicious opponent, one of the most evil I have ever faced and I am afraid that from the very beginning of this case back in 1902, I have underestimated the extent of his malevolent genius."

"My Kitty knew all about him," Porky ventured softly remembering the woman who had been so ill used by Gruner. "She knew the true measure of the man, his charming ways, but what a beast he truly was inside."

"I am sorry about Kitty," I said looking into Johnson's rough scarred face. "She was a true lady, someone quite special. She was brave to come forward and help me convince Violet De Merville about Gruner's true nature. I know she did it for revenge, but she was brave nevertheless."

Porky Shinwell rubbed some moisture from the corner of his eye, "Brave she was, Mr. 'Olmes. Aye, and with talk like that about her you'll have me bawling like a wee bairn before too long. But I does appreciate your good feelings about Kitty. She would be proud to hear them coming from someone like you. You know, she always thought highly of you, she did. While me Kitty could be a bad'n sometimes — it was in her nature like it is in me own I guess — she never did ill towards me and she never deserved the cards she was dealt."

I nodded; thinking of Kitty Winter caused my thoughts to drift to Watson. Was he, in fact, still alive? Dare I hope? Was he a prisoner of the wretched Baron? I was sure that he certainly must be. Was he in good health, or even now being tortured? It was maddening to contemplate but I struggled to put all these thoughts from my mind and concentrate on the work at hand. I was sure all would be made clear soon enough. One way or the other.

Our trap was fast approaching the outer gate of the wall that surrounded the estate of the Countess Von Huenfeld. I took a deep breath and looked at my companion, "Well now, Porky, are you ready?"

"Aye," he answered grimly, "ready as I'll ever be."

"Driver?" I told the man in a low voice. "You can stop here and let us off."

"'ere, sir? You don't want me to run you up to the 'ouse?"

"No," I replied. "Here is fine. We'll walk up to the house on our own. It's a lovely night for a walk."

"Walk, sir? It be quite a long walk."

"Here is just fine."

The driver shrugged, stopped the trap and Porky and I got out. I paid the man and a minute later he was gone and we stood alone at the outside wall that surrounded the expansive lawn of the huge estate.

"Lestrade and his men are behind us, they will be waiting for our signal," I stated softly. "We don't have much time before dawn and if we don't find Watson — dead or alive — we'll find ourselves back in gaol tomorrow, and it will be the rope for you that night."

"Aye, I can nary forget my appointment with the noose. It is one I do not want to keep if I can help it. It amazes me how a bare 24 hours can make such a difference in a man's fortunes," Johnson ruminated.

"No time for that now," I stated, focusing on our work. "Come, let's go."

We quickly climbed over the stone wall surrounding the estate and began our trudge towards the main house. It was a far walk, the estate was vast. We were ever watchful of sentries or guard dogs but luckily came across none. Thankfully this time there was no Hell Hound patrolling the grounds, such as I had encountered at Baskerville Hall.

It took us some time. The grounds were large and expansive, full of well manicured lawns, tightly cut trees and bushes, some trimmed into amazing topiary designs of animals and fish. There were also many Greek and Roman-inspired granite and limestone statues depicting graceful nymphs and spritely water dyads interspersed by small ponds full of large gold fish and covered with water lilies. All the accoutrements of wealth and excess I so detested.

"Blimey, Mr. 'Olmes, the place looks unreal…almost like — like heaven."

I smiled, obviously Porky had never seen the likes before. "The wealthy do have their fun. Can you see the house up ahead?"

"Aye, a mansion it be, for sure. So many bright lights it twinkles like a jewel," Porky whispered in awe.

"Come, let us get closer," I said and we walked on for what was a good five minutes more until we neared the main house.

"It's huge!" Porky said amazed. "How can we find the Doctor in that pile? I'd wager there are a thousand rooms there."

I smiled, "One-hundred and twenty rooms, which is quite enough for us. But do you notice anything strange about the building? Other than the size and opulence?"

"Op — u…?"

"The fancy nature of it," I explained with a grin.

"Yes, a lot of lights all over, except that one portion of it set in darkness."

"Exactly, Porky. An unused wing of the palace, steeped in darkness, no doubt closed off by the countess and her retinue. But why?" I said, my detective's nose taking up the scent and running with it. "Unless I miss my guess, that darkened wing of the house is where the Baron has located his secret quarters."

"So we head for it?"

"Yes, but careful now. Do you have your club?"

"All ready, sir, the Inspector himself gave it back to me," Porky hefted the stout piece of carved hard wood. "I tell you true, I can do more damage with a stout club than most layabouts can with a revolver."

"I do not doubt it," I told him. Meanwhile I felt the reassurance of the revolver in my coat pocket which Mycroft had given to me and insisted that I carry. I was thankful that I had it. I looked at Porky, "Let's go. We must find Watson — one way or the other!"

"Game's on, Mr. 'Olmes."

"Indeed it is, Mr. Johnson!"

Porky and I approached the mansion from the North side. That wing of the great house was steeped in darkness. This seemed to me the best location to make our entrance.

We trudged carefully between bushes and shrubs, over flower beds and between the many granite and limestone statues towards a set of large French windows ensconced in blackness.

"I know these, Mr. 'Olmes," Porky whispered, giving me a sly wink. "They opens up just like doors. Give me a second and I'll have them unlatched and us inside before you can say Raffles the cracksman was 'ere."

Porky was as good as his word, he jimmied the lock like the professional burglar he was. Then he and I opened the windows and stepped into the house to find ourselves in a long and dark hallway.

The place was flanked on both sides by more statues in the Ancient Greco-Roman style set upon pedestals and with large paintings of historic figures in ornate frames set upon the walls and looking down at us with arrogant regard. It was like some antiquities museum. I noticed the large double doors at both ends of the hall. They were closed and all remained dark and deathly quiet.

"What now?" Porky whispered, silently rubbing the club into the palm of his left hand. I'm afraid my companion was a bit impatient, all too ready and willing for some criminal class version of White Chapel payback. I did not feel it was my right to dissuade him from that task as of yet.

"The North wing was the dark part of the house so that is our target. Come, this way."

I led Porky to the end of the hallway which took us into the North wing of the house. We approached the large ornate double doors warily. I saw there was no manner of alarm there. I also looked for signs of light under the doors, or voices from inside the room. All indeed, seemed dark and quiet. It was most disconcerting. I tried the handle and found it unlocked, twisting it to release the closing mechanism, and then slowly opened the door.

Inside was pitch black and I could make out nothing, only that it was a large drawing room of some sort that seemed to stretch on endlessly. There didn't appear to be any furniture, but I noticed all the windows had been covered with heavy tapestries giving the entire room a veritable tomb-like appearance steeped in stygian darkness.

Porky and I slowly, silently walked into the room. It was indeed enormous. As my eyes became accustomed to the darkness I was finally able to make out something at the other end of the room about a hundred feet away from us. It looked like a large piece of furniture, or perhaps some kind of large black box.

Porky's eyes were younger than my own and he saw it clearly for what it was. He suddenly whispered to me ominously, "Blimey, it's a jail cell, I tell you, or a cage, and someone is in it."

Chapter 13
To The Rescue

I could make it out now too and my heart fairly leaped with joy. Was it Watson? Could it be him? Or was it just some poor unfortunate wretch that the Baron kept locked away here for his own personal amusement? Perhaps some missing girl from a local village, who he had abducted for his vile carnal pleasures?

"Come now," I urged my companion. "Careful."

We advanced quietly towards the cage. It was a small six foot square metal box made up of stout iron bars on all sides. There was a door and it was closed. I assume it was locked. I noticed a small cot set against the far side of the cage and upon it lay a bundle of something — something that appeared to be a man.

Porky and I silently approached the prisoner. Together as one, my companion and I reached between the bars and quickly held the man down firmly, making sure his mouth was covered so he could not cry out.

"Watson?" I whispered softly into the man's ear, hope daring to rise in my heart. "Watson, is it you?"

The man suddenly jumped awake, squirming, fighting, and still barely conscious. I could see now that the fellow had been made haggard by his captivity, but I recognized him at once and my heart leaped for joy.

It *was* Watson!

"Watson?" I whispered into his ear softly. "It is I, Sherlock. I have come for you. Be quiet now."

"Sherlock?" he muttered with awe, as if in utter disbelief. I carefully released my hand from his mouth.

"Yes, my friend, it is I, and I am here with Porky Johnson. We have come to rescue you." I stated. Porky let go his grip now which allowed

Watson the use of his hands. The good Doctor began to rub the sleep from his eyes and then sat up and looked at us in astonishment and sheer joy.

"Good God, Holmes, you are the last person I expected to see! I had almost given up hope. Is it truly you?"

"In the flesh, old man," I replied with a wide smile at seeing my friend alive. In fact, seeing Watson again proved a great boon to my aching heart. "Are you all right? Are you well? Uninjured?"

"Well enough, now that you are here," he replied softly with a tug at my shoulder.

"Yes, it is so good to see you. I almost gave up hope in those dark early days," I said.

"Well…well…you know, it is so very good to see you too," he stammered sternly trying to hold back tears.

"And I you, old friend."

"Ah, Mr. 'Olmes, time's ticking away," Porky reminded me.

"Quite right," I said focusing upon the problem at hand. "We must free Watson from his prison at once and then give Lestrade the signal."

"Hurry, Holmes!" Watson cried softly at the prospect of freedom. "They could be here any minute."

"How many of them are there?" I asked.

"Four total. Baron Gruner and three henchmen. One of them, Sergey, is enormous so be careful with him." Watson cautioned.

"We shall."

Suddenly the lights went on filling the room will brilliance. I saw four sinister figures at the other end of the room at the open doorway, all drawing revolvers and walking towards us. One of the figures wore a bizarre facial mask and I knew that he must be Baron Adelbert Gruner. They advanced slowly, warily, weapons trained upon us.

"I see I have two more trophies to add to my collection. Sergey, see to it that our guests are relieved of any weapons and then I will afford them accommodations with Doctor Watson," the Baron's muffled laughter cascaded with delight from behind his mask. "I am sure you have much to discuss."

Porky and I remained frozen. It appeared the game was up. We were lightly armed; Porky had only his wooden club and I had my small revolver, while Gruner and his three henchmen each held revolvers upon us. We were trapped, outgunned and we knew it.

"I'm sorry, Mr. 'Olmes," Porky told me, obviously broken-hearted as Gruner and his men continued to advance towards us, but I noticed

Johnson was still holding his club, holding it so tightly I could see his knuckles turning white.

"We're not in the stew yet," I whispered, for I noticed Gruner and his men seemed to be quite leery of us. They came forward but with great care and slowly. I had a sudden idea and whispered softly, "Let them get closer, then act upon my word."

Porky winked at me, "Got nothing to loose, so I'll take me chances with you."

"Good man," I told him. Then I turned to Watson, "Can you divert the attention of the closest one?"

"Yes."

"Wait for them to get closer, then attack upon my word."

The Baron and his men approached us warily; one would think they were the ones without weapons, so careful did they appear. In fact, they had been trained well. Perhaps former military, so they were naturally cautious, always watchful. Perhaps overly cautious? Or so I hoped.

"You! Drop the club!" one of the men ordered Porky in a thick Austrian accent, but my man refused to let go of his club even as the Baron's man threatened him with his gun.

"Sherlock Holmes," the Baron ruminated. "I do not know how you and this — thug criminal — escaped Scotland Yard, but I assure you, you will not escape my little prison so easily."

"Release Doctor Watson, immediately," I ordered.

The Baron laughed tersely, "It is I who command here, Mr. Holmes, not you. Never forget that." Then to his henchmen he barked the order, "Take them!"

The Baron's three henchmen moved fast to close with Porky and myself. I waited until they were almost upon Porky, then I gave the word.

"Now!" I shouted.

Instantly all was mayhem.

Everything transpired simultaneously and so quickly that to most people it would appear to have happened in a blur. Though for many it would be difficult to recall exactly just what happened, and in what order, here is the exact turn of events as they occurred. Upon my word first thing trusty Watson did was let fly with something through the bars of his cell. I realized that it was a book of all things, the hard spine of which hit the closest of Gruner's men square in the forehead. The thug was taken totally unawares by the blow, reeled backwards and dropped his revolver to the floor.

At the same instant, venerable Porky Johnson acted with speed and precision. Porky proved a man whose acumen with a club was no idle threat and he used it to knock the weapon out of the hand of the enormous Sergey, then braining the man with a harsh blow to the temple. He next let loose with a furious throw of that very club to hit the remaining thug in the face, knocking him senseless. Porky then quickly turned his attention back to the first thug, attacking Sergey before the big man had gotten his bearings. The two men were soon fiercely fighting for possession of Sergey's unattended revolver.

By that time I had already pulled my revolver from my pocket and put a bullet into the Baron's shoulder, causing him to drop his gun. Then I moved closer to cover Gruner and his other man with my revolver. The Baron and his two thugs were now under my control and I only awaited the outcome of the fight between Porky and Sergey.

At first I was not overly concerned with the outcome of the battle knowing Porky's criminal tendencies all too well and his ability to knock about an opponent, but soon things took a turn for the worse for my friend. Sergey was proving more than a match for Porky's hooligan skills.

Porky and Sergey were engaged in a fierce battle to determine who would take possession of Sergey's revolver. Both men now had their hands upon the weapon, even as each man pummeled the other ferociously. So close and so rapid was the combat that I dared not fire for fear of hitting Porky in the furious tumble, so I was relegated to a frustrated observer for the moment.

I knew that much relied on the outcome of this battle, and I knew I had to find some way to step in to even the odds in Porky's favor. Sergey was much larger than the tough but compact London hoodlum. I could see that my friend was now getting the worst of things from the Baron's larger and much younger henchman.

For a brief moment the sight caused me to reluctantly take my attention away from the Baron — he was wounded and the pain of his wound had incomododated him substantially — so I felt that was all the time I needed. I ran over to Porky, waited for a pause in the fight, then when I saw my opportunity I took the butt of my revolver and knocked Sergey hard upon the head.

The huge fellow collapsed into unconsciousness, covering Porky with his massive bulk like a blanket.

"Thanks, Mr. 'Olmes," I heard Porky mutter in a deep breath as he pushed the motionless body of Sergey off him.

"Bravo, Holmes!" I heard Watson cheer us from his cage.

I then helped Porky to his feet. He had Sergey's revolver so we were both armed now. Together we corralled the Baron and his three henchmen motioning them over to the cage where Watson was still held captive.

"Holmes, now please, get me out of here," Watson pleaded.

"Easy, old man, we'll get you out soon enough," I said, motioning the Baron and his men closer to the cage.

"The Baron has the only key," Watson informed me.

I looked to the Baron sternly, ordered him, "I will have that key now, Gruner."

"I'm afraid you will have to take it off my person, Mr. Holmes," he said defiantly through his face mask. "If you can ever find it, that is."

"Shoot him, Mr. 'Olmes! Put a bullet into his black heart. Kill him dead! Then take it off his corpse." Johnson advised sharply.

I ignored my friend's words. I'd not shoot Gruner in cold blood.

The Baron just let loose with a long, mocking laugh that from behind his mask sounded like the wailings of the doomed souls of a hundred Hells.

I walked over to the Baron, my revolver pointed straight at his heart. Perhaps Porky was correct? A bullet in the heart was certainly what the man deserved, but I held my hand, for I wanted to save Baron Gruner for better things. Notably a trial, and then a rope. But I didn't have to let him know that. So I shoved my face into his own and told him firmly, "I am not afraid to give you the justice you so richly deserve, Baron. You have been the cause of many innocent deaths, much evil."

"You talk quite grand, Mr. Sherlock Holmes with a gun in your hand," Gruner barked at me from behind his mask. "Let us see how bold you are without a weapon."

I smiled, he was baiting me, such a lame and hopeless attempt, but he'd soon find out that he would get more than he had bargained for. For I suddenly swung my hand at his head, using the revolver to knock loose the mask from his face and send it flying off to slide across the floor behind him.

Gruner screamed in shock and rage, using his hands to cover his hideous face — or what was left of it. I looked at him and lowered the revolver still in my hand.

"Now then, Baron, perhaps we are even," I told him as he cowered before me, his hands covering his disfigured face in shame. "You have no mask to cover your features and I have no revolver pointed at your heart."

We were frozen in time like that for a long moment.

"Don't do it, Holmes!" I heard Watson warn from his cage. "He's a tricky devil; the mask is just a ruse!"

"Smash him, Mr. 'Olmes," Porky cheered me on with murderous glee while he held his gun on the Baron's three henchmen. "If not you, then let me 'ave a crack at 'im. I'll rearrange that face quiet nicely, thank you."

Baron Gruner finally lowered his hands from his face and it was only then that I clearly saw the full import of what lay under his mask, and the full extent of the damage Kitty Winter had done to him with the vitriol years before. That once handsome face and form had been reduced to a grotesque mockery of something appearing human — or less than human. He was hideous and infernally grotesque. The acid had eaten away the skin and all pleasing features of his face, melting them into a mass of scarred black and blotted tissue, pestilent and putrescent, never able to heal or be whole again.

I saw Gruner's eyes had been reduced to two blood-red slits, the nose was entirely gone having been replaced by one large gaping hole in the center of his face, much like the blowhole of a whale. The mouth, sans lips, was twisted, with no teeth remaining. The ears had been totally eaten away as had most of the hair upon his once proud and handsome head — save several small ugly patches that hung limp, like dead seaweed. It was an altogether gruesome sight and I moved back a step shocked with revulsion, and dare I say it, almost with a pang of pity for the man and what had been done to him.

Almost.

For I reminded myself that all that had been done to the Baron was well deserved — truth be told he deserved far worse. I knew I had to ignore his grotesque disfigurement and remember that this man was a supremely dangerous criminal and brutal murderer.

Then, as if to validate those thoughts and prove me correct about the danger presented by the man, Gruner took advantage of an opportunity and suddenly changed his fortunes, and my own.

It happened this way.

I am afraid that my friend Porky's impatience that I should dispatch the Baron immediately had gotten the better of him. In wild anger he suddenly deserted the men he had been guarding and ran over to Gruner, quickly wrenching the man away from me.

Porky now held the Baron firmly in his grasp and was moving away from me, pressing his revolver into the neck of the man with a rage and hatred that was terrible to see.

"Now for you, my ugly Baron!" Porky growled in heated fury. "Now for Kitty too!"

"No, Porky!" I shouted, seeing that my companion was about to destroy all our hard work. "Don't do it, Porky! He must live to stand trial."

"Holmes! The Baron's men!" Watson barked in warning, for he saw that Porky's rash action had left them unattended and ready for mischief. I knew soon all would turn to chaos.

I tried to get close to Porky in a effort to take Gruner from him, but I realized that I had to keep all my attention on Gruner's three henchmen, since Porky had left them without a minder. They were now easing closer to us from three directions and threatened to outflank me.

My greatest fear was that Porky might execute Gruner right then and there, when all of a sudden everything changed.

Gruner produced a small revolver that must have been hidden upon his person. He fired the weapon and Porky fell back from the Baron in astonishment, dropping his own gun in wide-eyed shock. Porky had been shot in the side and now Gruner held my companion firmly by the neck with a gun to his own head.

"Porky!" I shouted in alarm. I ran over to him, but Gruner was too quick and motioned me away with his weapon.

"Back now, Mr. Holmes!"

I stopped frozen in my tracks, fearful of endangering my friend's life.

"Sorry, Mr. 'Olmes," Porky stammered. He was wounded and bleeding, but the wound did not look life-threatening. I was sure that the Baron's next shot would not be so compromising. He had wanted a hostage after all, and now he had one.

"So who has the upper hand now, Mr. Sherlock Holmes!" Gruner barked, his revolver pressed directly into Porky's head. I knew we had little choice in what was to come.

"Have a care!" Watson warned, but his warning came too late. The Baron held Porky firmly in his clutches. Speed and surprise had allowed him to get the drop on my companion, as our American friends would put it, and I silently I cursed Porky for an impatient fool while my mind raced to find some way out of this dreadful predicament.

"Mr. Holmes!" The Baron shouted to me. "Drop the gun or I shall kill your comrade."

"Don't do it!" Porky ordered me sternly. "My life means nothing to me now. Take your best shot and kill him, Mr. 'Olmes!"

"So who has the upper hand now, Mr. Sherlock Holmes!" Gruner barked.

"I shall kill your comrade, Mr. Holmes, if you do not surrender," Gruner demanded harshly, dragging Porky backwards towards his own men. "Then my men and I shall kill you too. You can not hope to prevail against all four of us."

I saw the truth of his words and it rankled me harshly.

I saw poor Porky looking at me regretfully. Then he said to the Baron, "Go ahead, you bloody bastard, do it! Mr. 'Olmes, shoot him down now! I don't care about my life."

"But I do!" I shouted boldly and saw Gruner's triumphant smile. I had no choice. Reluctantly I dropped my weapon to the ground.

Instantly the Baron's men took control of the situation, rearming themselves with the revolvers. Sergey relieved Porky of his beloved wooden club, using it on my companion's head a couple of times for added effect after the Baron placed Porky under Sergey's control.

The Baron's reversal had been neatly done and had changed everything now.

"And now, Mr. Holmes, I shall have all three of you placed in that cell under my power to do with as I please, for as long I please."

The Baron reached into his pocket and withdrew a key, throwing it to his main henchman. "Sergey, please open the cell, Doctor Watson is going to have two more guests."

Watson's jail cell was unlocked and Porky and I were unceremoniously thrown into the cage with the doctor.

"And there you'll stay, until Hell freezes over, or I decide to kill you," Gruner laughed oozing grim hateful bile. He staunched his wound and placed the mask back upon his face. Then he and his men left the room, slamming the doors behind them, leaving us alone.

Chapter 14
The Trap

*W*atson, Porky and I were quiet for a moment trying to understand just what had transpired and how our good fortunes could have sunk so quickly. How could things have gone so badly?

Well, Watson and I knew, but we remained mum about it.

"I'm so sorry, Mr. 'Olmes," Porky voiced his regret in a tone full of deep embarrassment. His rash move to take revenge for Kitty against the Baron had caused our downfall. "I was such a fool. Can you and the Doctor ever forgive me?"

I put my hand upon Porky's shoulder in staunch good fellowship, "Think nothing of it, my friend, and let us talk no further about it. Rather than offer recrimination, let us work to extricate ourselves from this situation."

"Baron Gruner's a tricky devil," Watson stated. "I fear that we all have underestimated him."

"Yes, I agree. I'm afraid it is my error, for I underestimated the man from the very beginning."

"No, Holmes, do not hold anything against yourself. No man, not even Sherlock Holmes himself, could ever plumb the length and depth of that man's insidious evil," Watson told me firmly.

"Thank you, Watson." His words surely buoyed my spirits.

Watson smiled at me, "Well, at least you are here now. It is good to see you."

"And I you, old friend." I added with a wry grin. "I am also happy to note that the reports of your demise have been greatly exaggerated."

Watson laughed out loud at that, "No one is happier about that news than I."

I shook Watson's hand warmly; it was good to have him back.

"One more thing, Mr. 'Olmes," Porky reminded me. "I'm afraid we never got the signal off to the Inspector,"

"Lestrade?" Watson looked at me in surprise. "He is here?"

I nodded. Then I briefly explained what the situation was regarding any rescue by the Inspector and the official police. I finished up by telling Watson, "Lestrade and his men are waiting for word from us, but the Yard will not risk an international incident by raiding the home of the countess without conclusive evidence produced. I'm afraid that evidence is you, old man."

"I see," Watson said glumly.

"Well, at any rate I'll be missing my date with the hangman's noose," Porky reminded me with a wry grin. "It's no shame at all, for I've grown accustomed to me neck, and to me life."

I nodded absently, looking away from my two companions, thinking of our ultimate fate if we did not discover a way out of Watson's small six foot square iron cage. I looked at Porky, "Can you pick this lock?"

"Not unless I have proper tools. It looks to be a quality mechanism," my criminous friend replied with a hangdog look of defeat.

I nodded, reaching into the band of my trousers where I pulled out some flexible and slim metal picks that I had secreted there. More gifts from brother Mycroft. I handed them to Porky. "Can you use these?"

"Blimey, Mr. 'Olmes, you does come prepared," he said with a wide grin as he took the picks and looked them over approvingly. "Aye, these might just do the trick."

Then Johnson got to work. He inserted three of the thin flexible metal picks into the lock keyhole, manipulating them through the bars from the outside like the master criminal craftsmen he was. It was tight work, difficult to judge the effect of his movements from his place behind the locking mechanism.

"Here," Watson said, bringing over a small shaving mirror he had with his personal kit. He deftly held the mirror outside the bars placing it at such an angle that Porky could now see exactly how his picks were affecting the workings of the lock.

"Very good, Doctor. That's certainly a help," the wily criminal said with a grimace as he renewed his efforts upon the lock.

Watson and I were quiet as we watched Porky continue his work.

"Not one of me easier jobs, sirs," Porky allowed after a moment, but there was confidence in his voice now. "These locks are stubborn, that's why the police and the likes use 'em so often, but I think… Yes, I hear movement inside now. I think… I'm…getting…it."

Suddenly there was a telltale click. Porky looked at me and I looked over at Watson. Dare we hope? Porky carefully pushed on the cell door and we were rewarded to see it slowly open outward.

"Finally!" Watson said in stark relief. Now he walked out of his cell, a free man for the first time in many weeks. "Free at last!"

Porky and I followed at his heels.

"Good job," I told our criminal companion.

"Years of practice, sir. I only hope it went some way in making up for me earlier foolishness that got us into this mess in the first place," Porky said demurely.

"You have done well, Shinwell Johnson," I told the man. "You have done very well, indeed! Thank you."

"Yes, good job, Mr. Johnson," Watson added, patting Porky upon his back.

"Ah, Mr. 'Olmes…Ah…Doctor…"

"Now what?" Watson asked me.

"Now we take down the Baron," I said simply. "We lay our trap for him. Porky, can you back track the way we got here, go to the gate and give Lestrade the signal for his men to raid the house? Can you do it with that shoulder wound? Watson can take a look at it, if need be."

"No, I'm fine, sir," Porky replied with verve. "Yes, I can do it."

"Good, then Doctor Watson and I will hold off Baron Gruner and his men until you return with Lestrade and his men."

"Well, that's fine I'm sure, but I was 'oping to join in the fight with you, Mr. 'Olmes…" Porky asked demurely. "For Kitty, you know…?"

"I understand, but I need you to go and give the signal."

"Yes, of course, I will do it!"

"Good man! I promise you, you'll have your revenge and Kitty will have hers too, once the Baron is placed in the dock and hung for his crimes. Now be off, and give Lestrade that signal before it is too late."

"Aye, sir," and our friend ran to the window, quickly escaping out of the room into the gloom of night to be gone in an instant.

Chapter 15
To Catch A Villain

"Well, it will take Porky some time to reach Lestrade, and more time for Lestrade and his men to get back here and begin the raid," I told Watson. "It looks like it is just you and me now, old friend. Are you up to it?"

"You know that I am, Holmes."

"Stout fellow! I never doubted you for a moment. We'll beard this Austrian beast in his own den yet! Come now, let us set ourselves ready to trap them should they come back here," I said boldly. "For if I know Gruner, he surely will come back here to gloat over us before the night is done."

"Yes, he is of that nefarious type," Watson admitted sternly. Then he looked at me curiously and asked, "But, Holmes, how *did* you know I was alive? And how were you able to get Lestrade to go along with your plan?"

I smiled at my companion. We were positioned on each side of the large double doors at the end of the room. Should the Baron, or any of his men, decide to enter we would easily have the drop on them. At present all was quiet and it appeared that we had some time to spare, so I decided to put it to good use by answering some of Watson's questions.

"It was a close run thing I can tell you, my friend," I explained *sotto voce*. "Mycroft helped. The Baron pulled a neat trick and almost got away with it. Your double appeared to be the spitting image of yourself, right down to your military wound. I expect the Baron expended considerable time and effort to find the perfect candidate, but then I am sure he planned this scheme for some time. Perhaps years. It was upon the examination of your dental records that Mycroft was able to prove conclusively that the man in the grave of Doctor Watson was *not* Doctor Watson!"

"Dental records? Who would have thought? That's amazing, Holmes!"

"Elementary, my friend," I said with a wry grin. "It was Mycroft's idea. Regardless, that evidence changed everything, leading to many questions for which Inspector Lestrade had no answers. These types of nagging questions bother men like my brother and Lestrade. Mycroft's man, Morgan, had suspicions the Baron was here in Kent, hiding in the retinue of the Dowager Countess Alexa Von Huenfeld. She is, by the way, unaware of all this plotting and criminal behavior being done in her home, but being the older sister of the German Kaiser it made the situation fraught with delicate international political considerations. That made any official action very complicated. Mycroft could act, but he needed conclusive evidence."

"But how could he and Lestrade be so sure? They were gambling so much on this plan, their very careers perhaps, if they were proved wrong." Watson stated.

"We were all as sure as we could be under the circumstances," I added glumly, it had been a long, hard road. "But you see; Mycroft had contingency plans for every eventuality. However, it is you who are the key here, my good Watson. You are the evidence we desperately need. That's why the police are awaiting the signal. If Porky and I found you then Lestrade and his men would come in and round up the Baron and his men."

"I see, but if you did not find me?"

"That's quite a different matter. I am afraid that then another part of the plan would kick in. Porky and I would have no choice but to turn ourselves in to Lestrade and be returned to gaol. Then events would proceed as originally scheduled, first with Johnson's execution. Then with my trial for your murder. Oh, I am sure I could beat that charge now, with what we know, but by that time it would certainly not help poor Porky."

"I see. So what now? What will happen?"

I gave my friend a grim but hopeful look, "Porky will reach Lestrade and tell him that you are alive, which means we have our evidence against the Baron. Then the inspector and his men will raid the house. However, if something goes wrong he may still put forth the story the police were alerted that two escapees from Hunston Prison were seen lurking on the estate of the Countess Von Huenfeld and had been apprehended."

Watson shook his head, "It seems complicated."

"Yes, I know, but we needed a complicated plan to defeat a complicated plan. The results will soon be made public how you were discovered a prisoner in the home of the countess and freed. Then you will become the key witness against Baron Gruner and all his crimes. Your statement on the affair of your abduction and captivity will also clear myself, and hopefully stall Porky's execution. Or such is the plan."

"Then Lestrade's men should be here soon?" Watson asked hopefully. I could see that he had been through a long nightmare which he hoped was at last coming to an end.

"Soon, Watson, be patient, my friend," I said softly.

Watson certainly looked none the worse for wear on first appearance. It was obvious the Baron had not physically abused or tortured him, as I had first feared, but the torment and emotional turmoil placed upon him by his imprisonment had caused him to appear worn and haggard. Nevertheless, my old friend kept a stiff upper lip; the epitome of determination and the tough British bulldog.

"Stout old Watson! It is so good to see you again, my friend. I so much feared for you. I could never really accept the fact that you were dead, but for those dark moments in the beginning I must admit the shock and evidence did confuse me. Even worse, the evidence placed by the Baron to prove my guilt made it impossible for me to be set free on bail to find him, or save you. It absolutely convinced Lestrade in the beginning, as it was meant to do. That tied me up quite neatly and made me unable to act as I should have."

"I know. I read about it in the papers, it was terrible," Watson replied with a wan smile. "I feared for your life, as well, not to mention your very reputation. Your magnificent career. I followed it each day in the daily papers. Baron Gruner, in his pompous arrogance, made sure I was kept up to date with all the sordid news. He had a perverse pleasure in my rage and frustration when I read about your plight."

"Yes, a truly evil man. He must be brought down."

"Soon, Holmes?"

"Yes, Watson, soon," I said softly as we continued our guard duty.

Suddenly we heard footsteps approaching the outer door, then we heard them in the outside hallway coming closer.

I looked at Watson and he nodded knowingly. It was time to spring our trap and catch this monster in his own den. We readied ourselves.

The large double doors soon opened and one of the Baron's henchmen walked into the room. Immediately Watson set upon him. The man never expected the attack and the good doctor hit him hard and quickly, while I disarmed him. Watson had given the thug a well-placed, one-two punch to the chin that put him down and out flat on his back upon the floor. It was nicely done.

"Where did you learn that?" I asked, pleasantly surprised by my companion's latent pugilistic skills.

"India, of course, in the Army. I did some boxing back then in my younger days. It seems one never knows when that type of thing might come in useful."

"Well, bravo!" I smiled, handing the thug's revolver to my friend, "Here, now things are a little more evenly matched."

I tied up the man with strips of cloth and gagged him securely.

Some time passed. It appeared the Baron's henchman was not missed, for no one else followed him into the room to confront us and everything remained quiet throughout the house for the next twenty minutes. I wondered what had become of Porky. Surely he should have reached Lestrade by now?

Suddenly we were startled to hear a loud gunshot from outside the house, from somewhere out upon the vast lawn. In response we heard three more gunshots. Then all was quiet once again. My heart fell to my feet at these sounds and what they might portend.

"Johnson?" Watson asked fearfully.

"I fear they have discovered him."

"Perhaps it is Lestrade and his men beginning their raid?" Watson asked hopefully.

I shook my head. "No, I'm afraid we must accept the fact that our friend, Porky, has failed."

Not soon afterwards the Baron himself with one of his men strode into the room. We were in no mood for niceties by then. Watson immediately took aim and let off a gunshot that dropped Gruner's man to the floor with a bleeding chest wound. I quickly flung myself in a wild attack upon the Baron, knocking him to the ground. The two of us rolled around in a wild melee. We were soon engaged in a furious battle as I tried to take the gun out of Gruner's hand.

Suddenly the third and last of Gruner's henchmen entered the room, took in what was happening in an instant and ran to help his master. It was the enormous brute, Sergey.

Sergey quickly got off a shot that dropped Watson to the ground.

Then he came for me.

"Watson!"

I struggled with the Baron, terrified now that my old comrade might be dying before my eyes. I wanted to rush to his aid but I was so entangled with Gruner that before long I found myself fighting for my very life. All of a sudden I felt my head being pummeled with something hard, the butt of a revolver held in Sergey's massive hand. Then I grew groggy, helpless, senseless.

I felt the Baron push me off him with disdain and rage. Now I lay upon the floor, still conscious but stunned, my eyes trying to focus on Watson and wondering why he did not move. I recalled that he had been shot but I prayed that it was not serious. I shouted his name, but he did not answer me. However, the Baron did.

"Never fear, Mr. Holmes," Gruner said, now standing tall in victory over Watson and myself; his henchman Sergey, beside him pointing a gun down at us.

"Watson?" I shouted.

There was no reply.

The Baron rearranged his clothing and reset the mask upon his face that had been knocked off in our struggle. Then he came close to me and pointed his weapon down at my head. He growled in a mocking tone, "You have caused me considerable trouble, Mr. Holmes, but it is of no consequence I assure you. Your criminal associate, Mr. Johnson, is dead. My man shot him down at the gate. However your appearance here has caused me considerable concern. I have decided to clear up everything regarding the two of you here and now before I take my leave of England for good."

Baron Gruner stood motionless, pointing his gun down at my head.

"If you kill me here in the home of the countess you will find you will have a lot to explain to the authorities, and that noble lady."

"I do not think so. That would be the case only should anyone ever find your body, Mr. Holmes. Which I can assure you, they will not. But fear not, detective Holmes, you are not to die — at least not yet. You shall live a little longer, just long enough to watch me empty this weapon into the body of your friend and companion, Doctor Watson. And in doing so, I shall get my final revenge upon him — *and upon you!*"

"No!" I shouted.

"Now, Mr. Holmes, prepare for the true murder of Doctor Watson!"

The die was cast. Sergey stood over me with his revolver trained upon me, rendering me helpless, as the Baron slowly walked over towards Watson. Gruner was playing his ghastly little game for all it was worth. He was purposely elongating the murderous process with evident sadistic glee.

Gruner took his time but eventually he stood defiantly over the doctor's prone and motionless form. I froze, expecting at any second the Baron would begin firing his weapon into poor Watson, but then the man did something I never expected at all. With almost theatrical effect, he carefully took off his facial mask and bent down close to the prone form of Watson to be sure my friend saw every detail of his hideous face.

"Look at me, Doctor Watson!" Gruner demanded in a loud gush of twisted evil rage. "Look at me now, and let my face be the last thing that you see before you die!"

It was then that the gun fired.

Or more accurately — *a* gun fired.

I instantly realized that the report had not come from Gruner's weapon at all, or from his henchman, Sergey.

The report had come from another source. Another weapon.

Then there was a second shot. Then the click of a now empty gun.

I quickly turned and saw Shinwell "Porky" Johnson with a smoking gun in his hand, a man who had apparently returned from the grave. I was stunned to see Porky, his form a mass of dripping bloody wounds. His second gunshot had squarely hit the man guarding me, the giant Sergey. Sergey clutched his chest and fell to the floor.

Next Porky threw himself in a running leap to land atop the prone form of Doctor Watson. He landed precisely at the moment when Baron Gruner began to empty his gun into the body of the man below him.

It was chaotic, shocking, the bullets from Gruner's gun poured into the man below him — but by then it was *not* Watson's body — it was Porky's body! Porky, who had already been shot and God alone knew how he had made it back here, now had saved Watson and myself with his valiant actions.

He took six slugs from the Baron's revolver.

"Porky!" I shouted, quickly firing my weapon and putting a slug into the Baron's hand. That caused him to drop his now empty gun to the ground. Nevertheless, the damage had been done. I ran over to Porky.

"I did it, Mr. 'Olmes! I got the signal out!" I heard Porky shout then, between muffled and bloody gasps of breath. "Lestrade is on the way, you and the Doctor will be safe now."

"Porky!" I cried, holding his bloody form close to me.

"Oh, my God, it is Mr. Johnson!" Watson muttered. He had just resumed consciousness and now realized what had happened.

"Say a prayer for Kitty and me, good sirs," Porky coughed blood now. Then he looked away and above him and whispered softly, "I'm on the way to you, my love, so save a spot for old Porky at your side."

Then Shinwell "Porky" Johnson died.

"No!" Watson shouted in rage.

"Porky!" I cried, full of anger and sadness. At that point I am afraid that blind rage had taken its hold over me for I stood up and I calmly walked over to the Baron as if I were some kind of mindless automaton. My hands grabbed Gruner, wrapping themselves around his throat, and I began to squeeze the life out of him.

"For all the evil you have wrought, you shall die by my own hands, my bloody Baron!"

Baron Gruner gasped for each breath, his horrid face, so close to my own, seemed to grow even more gruesome if that was possible, while my hands relentlessly squeezed the very life out of him. He did not cry out, nor even plead for mercy — though I am sure he knew he could expect no such boon from me after all he had done. Once, when he could summon the effort and grasp a halting breath, he did laugh at me, wildly, insanely, defiantly. It was utterly chilling.

"Holmes! Holmes, stop it!" I heard Watson shout. He had come up behind me and was trying to pull my hands away from the Baron's throat. "Stop, you'll kill him!"

"That is my intention."

"No, do not do it!"

"He deserves death!" I explained, pushing Watson away from me, but my friend was a relentless fellow and came back at me like the bulldog he was.

"I agree, I agree, but there's a rope waiting for him, Holmes! *A rope!* Hold off, please, at least for Porky and Kitty!"

I froze at Watson's words, looked from Gruner's evil distorted face into the wholesome goodness of Watson's compassionate gaze. I sighed deeply, relaxed my grip a bit, "It has been a long and terrible journey, my friend."

"Holmes, Lestrade and his men are here now. You can release your grip on Baron Gruner. Let the official police take over. You've done more than any man could ever do," then Watson gently pulled my hands from the Baron's throat.

"Porky, did more," I growled defiantly.

"That he did, and he'll not be forgotten for it. Now he's with Kitty. I know he is finally happy. The world was never the same for him, once she was taken from it," Watson told me as I allowed him to ease my fingers from Gruner's throat. "Come now, Holmes, release your grip and let Lestrade and the police take care of this creature."

I looked at my old friend closely, offering him a wry grin, "So be it, good Watson, I yield to your humanity."

"Not humanity, Holmes, but justice." he told me sharply. "Firm British Justice!"

"Yes, right you are as ever, old man."

"Mr. Holmes?"

"Ah, Lestrade," I replied with some of my old bluster having returned, for I noticed the Inspector and his men had just arrived. "Here is one you will want to put into safe keeping. Allow me to present Baron Adelbert Gruner, found at last upon firm British soil. He is the man responsible for the murder of Kitty Winter, Simon Germain, Shank Frobish, Shinwell "Porky" Johnson, the unfortunate substitute Watson who still remains unidentified, as well as the abduction and captivity of the real Watson and the framing of myself for murder. It is quite a long list of misdeeds. A rope is hungry for his neck."

"Indeed, Mr. Holmes," Lestrade said, as he and his men rushed over. "You have done it! You have saved Doctor Watson!"

"He has saved us both," Watson said stoutly.

I didn't acknowledge their words but I did release a gasping Baron Gruner into the hands of Lestrade's men, who were noticeably appalled and shocked when they got a good look at the grotesque face of the Baron.

"He is all yours now, Lestrade. Yours for a hangman's noose."

Lestrade shook his head, "Well, will you look at him! He's certainly the ugly little creature, but for all the evil he's done he'll pay the proper price now. Even hanging may be too good for you, Baron. Constables, take that man away."

Chapter 16
Back At Baker Street

urning logs sputtered melodically in our fireplace as they warmed the common area that I shared with Doctor John H. Watson at Baker Street. The two of us, along with my brother, Mycroft, had lately been joined by Inspector Lestrade of Scotland Yard. The warm glow from the fire, aided by some lubrication brought about by the liberal use of a more than adequate brandy, did much to lighten our moods after the events of the last few weeks. The long nightmare was finally over and the Baron Gruner case was closed.

Of course by then I had been cleared of all charges of Watson's murder. Better yet, the popular press had done a veritable *mea culpa* and now steadfastly lauded my deductive methods, even as they examined every aspect of Baron Gruner and his insidious plot to destroy Watson and myself. Now the popular press printed stories that lauded me as some type of hero and praised my deductive methods as nothing short of miraculous.

Hah!

Of course Watson and I made sure that Shinwell "Porky" Johnson and Kitty Winter were not forgotten in these press accounts. Porky's bravery and bold self-sacrifice held banner headlines in newspaper stories and became the stuff of legend, while their ill-fated love story made even old maids weep.

With all the good news for myself; Watson also had much to be thankful for. He had finally been freed from his torment and imprisonment and was now once again safely ensconced at Baker Street with me, where he belonged.

Meanwhile, Baron Adelbert Gruner was in prison awaiting trial for multiple murders. This time, no doubt, he would receive a date with the hangman's noose which was so justly deserved for his hideous crimes.

Mycroft uneasily voiced to us his concerns upon that score, but Watson was confident in the steadfastness of good, firm British justice.

I held my tongue.

"He nearly had you, Mr. Holmes," this from Inspector Lestrade, who now spoke up from between sips of brandy. "The evidence against you was very neatly done."

I just smiled without comment. I did not want to relive how close we had all come to disaster. Finally I told him, "In the end it proved a close run thing, indeed."

"Well, I for one am overjoyed to be free of that damnable cage and that evil monster leering at me from behind that grotesque mask and mocking me to no end. I still see him in my dreams haunting me," Watson blurted, refilling his glass with a bit more brandy than was his usual.

"Political complications aside," Mycroft added reluctantly, "the Dowager Countess Von Huenfeld had no idea at all that her Austrian nephew had caused so much havoc. Once notified, she was outraged and visibly shaken by the news. I have heard that she has disowned her nephew and all his actions. Which means, I imagine, that Baron Gruner has lost the support he may once have enjoyed from the Austrian royal family. He's very neatly in the soup and almost cooked."

"Then all has ended well," Watson said, as my brother and Lestrade nodded their heads in agreement.

I said nothing but stood up from my chair and began to pace the room restlessly. "There is a sadness in your face, Holmes," Watson asked. "What is it?"

"Yes, what troubles you, Sherlock?" my brother added.

I shook my head with deep regret, "I can not help but think about poor Porky and Kitty. I would like to think they are together again, just as Porky had wished, and in a better place."

"Yes, I agree," Watson said softly. "I am sure that they are."

"Well now, little brother, that's quite an emotional statement and rather unlike you at all," Mycroft said, looking at me with raised eyebrows.

I smiled at my older brother, "Why, Mycroft, I can be quite the emotional fellow on occasion, especially where true love is concerned. Isn't that true, Watson?"

Watson looked at me rather startled by my words, "Well…ah… I imagine so, Holmes, but I'm not sure I know exactly what you mean…"

I laughed heartily, my eyes misting with emotion, "Watson, good old,

Watson, you are priceless! I tell you now; I feared I had lost you forever. It was terrible to contemplate your death. You are not just a friend, but as a brother to me, and dare I say it, loved like a brother as well. John, it is good to have you back among the living."

"Well, er...thank you, Holmes...Sherlock... I must say no one more than I is happier to be back among the living...I mean...I certainly hope so!"

Epilogue
A Visit From Mycroft

"Where are my morning papers?" I bellowed from our sitting room in a voice that rang throughout the building of 221 and fairly threatened to knock it down around me. "Mrs. Hudson! I left explicit instructions that all daily newspapers were to be left here on this very table every morning. Watson, have you seen them?"

"I…well…ah…" he stammered so unconvincingly that I knew something was up.

"Watson?"

"Yes, Holmes?"

"You are hiding the newspapers from me. Now why would you do such a thing?"

"Well…" he sighed deeply, and I could see anger and frustration playing upon his face. He shook his head, for he had been found out and now there was nothing for him to do but come clean with me about what he had done.

"Well?" I prompted impatiently.

Watson did not answer.

I looked at my friend sternly; ready to give him a firm admonishment, when I was suddenly alerted by heavy footfalls upon the steps leading to our rooms. Of course I recognized those footsteps only too well. Now what?

My brother entered our rooms solemnly. I could see he was much distressed.

"Mycroft?" I asked carefully. "What are you doing here?"

"I have news, Sherlock."

"Gruner?"

Mycroft sighed. He did not take off his coat or hat. I saw that this would be a short visit and not at all a social call. It was official Empire business, distasteful, direct and to the point. "I wanted to tell you before you read it in the papers. A deal has been made."

"A deal!" I fairly shrieked the words as my anger exploded.

"Easy now," my brother admonished.

"You allowed him to slip through your fingers!"

"Now, Sherlock!"

I fumed but remained silent for the moment, awaiting an explanation. Watson stood by in open-mouthed shock.

"I know you will not like this outcome, gentlemen, and I am not overly approving of it myself, but it is what must be done. Baron Gruner has been set free. After all, we could hardly execute a member of the Austrian Royal Family, now could we? That would only precipitate international complications of the most dire sort. Perhaps even war. A war we have tried to forestall for many years. There was no other alternative."

It was one of the few times in my life when I found myself at a loss for words. I felt betrayed by my own brother and his baroque political machinations.

Mycroft quickly explained, "Baron Gruner is a nephew of the German Kaiser's older sister, hence his own nephew as well. Furthermore, through the Kaiser he has certain familial relations with our own King Edward. There could be no other outcome with such connections. However, we do have the steadfast assurance of the Austrian and German governments that the Baron will never set foot in the United Kingdom or any of its territories or colonies ever again."

"And you believe that?" I said, my voice dripping sarcasm.

"It is not a matter of what I believe, Sherlock. I do not expect you to approve of what had to be done to keep the peace, but I do hope you will accept it"

"Well I think this is simply outrageous!" Watson blurted in red-faced anger. "It stinks of politics!"

"Might I remind you, Doctor Watson, that it was through 'politics' — deal making and favors owed — by which I was able to obtain my brother's release from his cell in Scotland Yard in order to effect your rescue, as well as capture the Baron, in the first place," Mycroft stated curtly.

"In truth, I feared some such outcome," I replied looking away from my brother, a pall of defeat entering my mood.

"I am sorry, Sherlock," Mycroft told me.

"As am I mightily disappointed, Mycroft. I am aware of the political sensitivities involved in the Gruner case, and I am sure you are doing what you feel you must to protect the Empire and keep the peace. I do not agree with it, but I will accept it. However, you may find that the deal you have struck here this day will come back to haunt you by precipitating the very situation you have tried to forestall. You are playing with fire."

My brother looked at me intently and for a fleeting instance I saw doubt then alarm flicker across his features. Then it was gone, replaced by his cold professional countenance.

"What will happen now?" Watson asked in obvious frustration.

"The Baron is already on his way back to Austria. We will never see him again," Mycroft stated. "He may have escaped justice, but you both escaped his plan for revenge. At least that has been thwarted."

"Not so," I offered glumly. "Kitty Winter and Porky Johnson are still dead. As are others. Where is their justice?"

Mycroft nodded sadly, "That is true. Some day we shall make the Baron pay for those crimes. I pray for that day. However, now, I must be off. I am due back at Whitehall on urgent business. Once again, I am sorry it turned out this way, Sherlock, truly I am, but there was no other outcome possible. This is the way it must work out."

After my brother left our rooms Watson and I sat alone in quiet thought. The silence of anger and defeat was so overwhelming neither of us could speak a word until Mrs. Hudson came to us with the telegram. She handed the envelope to the doctor and then walked out.

I winced at what it might contain, "Open it, Watson. Read it to me, please."

The doctor took the message, opened it up, scanning the contents with care. A grim look overcame his face.

"Perhaps you should see this, Holmes."

I tore the paper from Watson's fingers and read words written there that shall forever burn within my heart. It was a simple, short note, and all it said was:

Once again it appears we end in stalemate.
The next time you shall not be so fortunate, I assure you.
Until we meet again, Mr. Sherlock Holmes.
—- Baron Adelbert Gruner von Huenfeld

I tore the paper from Watson's fingers and read words written there that shall forever burn within my heart.

About our Creators

Author -
GARY LOVISI is a Mystery Writer's of America Edgar Nominated author for his Sherlock Holmes pastiche, "The Adventure of the Missing Detective." He is an avid Sherlockian, as well as writer and book collector. His latest books are *More Secret Adventures of Sherlock Holmes* (Ramble House, 2011) a collection of three new Holmes pastiche stories, *Bad Girls Need Love Too* (Krause, 2010), a celebration of pulp paperback cover art, and *Ultra-Boiled* (Ramble House, 2010), a collection of 23 intense, hard crime and noir stories. Lovisi is the founder of Gryphon Books, editor of *Paperback Parade* and *Hardboiled* magazines, and sponsors an annual book collector show in New York City. To find out more about him, his work, or Gryphon Books, visit his web site at: www.gryphonbooks.com.

Interior Illustrator –
ROB DAVIS is a freelance artist and Art Director for Airship 27. He is the winner of the 2009 Pulp Factory award for Best Interior Illustration. Since his professional debut in 1987 Rob's work has appeared in comic books from a diverse list of publishers including Marvel and DC, specialty newspapers, T-shirt designs as well as numerous New Pulp books from the aforementioned Airship 27. He lives in the rural wooded hills of mid-Missouri with his wife, two children, two cats and a dog. Check out his work at robmdavis.com

THE BAKER STREET SLEUTH RETURNS!

Made in the USA
Las Vegas, NV
22 February 2022

44390297R00085